GIRL MEETS GHOST

Don't miss these other great books
by Lauren Barnholdt:

Fake Me a Match

Rules for Secret Keeping

Devon Delaney Should Totally Know Better

Four Truths and a Lie

The Secret Identity of Devon Delaney

GIRL MEETS GHOST

LAUREN BARNHOLDT

Aladdin

NEW YORK LONDON TORONTO SYDNEY NEW DELHI

If you purchased this book without a cover, you should be aware that this book is stolen property. It was reported as "unsold and destroyed" to the publisher, and neither the author nor the publisher has received any payment for this "stripped book."

This book is a work of fiction. Any references to historical events, real people, or real places are used fictitiously. Other names, characters, places, and events are products of the author's imagination, and any resemblance to actual events or places or persons, living or dead, is entirely coincidental.

✎ ALADDIN

An imprint of Simon & Schuster Children's Publishing Division
1230 Avenue of the Americas, New York, NY 10020
First Aladdin paperback edition August 2013
Copyright © 2013 by Lauren Barnholdt
All rights reserved, including the right of reproduction in whole or in part in any form.
ALADDIN is a trademark of Simon & Schuster, Inc., and related logo is a
registered trademark of Simon & Schuster, Inc.
Also available in an Aladdin hardcover edition.
For information about special discounts for bulk purchases, please contact
Simon & Schuster Special Sales at 1-866-506-1949 or business@simonandschuster.com.
The Simon & Schuster Speakers Bureau can bring authors to your live event. For more
information or to book an event, contact the Simon & Schuster Speakers Bureau
at 1-866-248-3049 or visit our website at www.simonspeakers.com.
The text of this book was set in Minion.
Manufactured in the United States of America 0913 OFF
10 9 8 7 6 5 4 3 2
The Library of Congress has cataloged the hardcover edition as follows:
Barnholdt, Lauren.
Girl meets ghost / by Lauren Barnholdt. — First Aladdin hardcover edition.
p. cm.
Summary: Seventh-grader Kendall can see dead people. Not only can she see them, she
can speak to them . . . and they can speak to her. They want Kendall to be a psychic sleuth
and figure out what unresolved issues are keeping them from moving on.
ISBN 978-1-4424-4246-7 (hc)
[1. Dead—Fiction. 2. Ghosts—Fiction. 3. Psychic ability—Fiction. 4. Middle schools—
Fiction. 5. Schools—Fiction. 6. Mystery and detective stories.] I. Title.
PZ7.B2667Gi 2013
[Fic]—dc23
2012032234
ISBN 978-1-4424-2146-2 (pbk)
ISBN 978-1-4424-2149-3 (eBook)

For Krissi,
who makes me proud to be her sister

Acknowledgments

A million billion thank-yous to:

My awesome editor, Fiona Simpson, for taking over and not skipping a beat! This book would not be what it is if it weren't for your amazing insight and advice.

My agent, Alyssa Eisner Henkin, for being the best agent a girl could ask for. Alyssa, I can't imagine doing what I do without you. Thank you for everything.

Kate Angelella, for coming up with the idea and believing in me enough to think I could do it. I miss you!!!

My mom, for always passing out my books to any random person she can think of. Mom, you've always believed in me, and for that I am forever grateful.

My sister Kels, for writing with me, making me laugh, and being the best friend and sister in the whole entire world.

Jessica Burkhart, for being a great friend. Love our #1k1hr sessions on Twitter—thanks for always listening to me and being there to talk writing or life! Team Barnhart FTW. <3

Kevin Cregg, for sending me song recommendations and taking me to Big Dip all those years ago.

My dad and Beth, for their support.

Everyone at Simon & Schuster for all the amazing things you do for me and my books.

And finally, my husband, for everything. Aaron, you're the most amazing thing that's ever happened to me, and every single day I thank God I'm lucky enough to have someone like you in my life. Thanks for making me a better person, a better writer, and making me believe in fairy tales. I love you.

Chapter

1

You know how sometimes you're doing something totally important, like picking out the perfect Stila lip gloss, or staring at the back of Brandon Dunham's neck during math (trust me, he has a very cute neck), and you get interrupted by something horribly annoying, like an unwanted text message or a teacher calling on you? Yeah, welcome to my world. Only, a lot of the time it's not my phone or a teacher interrupting me. A lot of the time it's a ghost. I see them. I listen to them. And then I do whatever they tell me so that they can get closure and move on to wherever it is ghosts go.

Like right now, for example. I'm in math, and this girl ghost (usually the ghosts are girls—I'm not sure why that is, and it's not like I can ask someone what the rules are) just shows up, dressed like a gymnast, and starts doing cartwheels and flips! Right down the aisle between the rows of desks!

Of course she's blond (figures), around sixteen (figures), and really beautiful (figures, figures, figures). She's all, "Kendall, help me!"

And my dad wonders why my math grades are so bad. It's because of distractions like this (and Brandon Dunham's neck, which, as previously mentioned, is very, very nice).

"Kendall Williams?" my math teacher, Mr. Jacobi, says from the front of the room.

"I'm sorry," I say in my most polite tone. "Can you repeat the number of the problem you'd like answered?"

"I don't want a problem answered," Mr. Jacobi says. "I want you to tell me what you got on your quiz, so that I can record it in my grade book."

"Oh," I say. "Um, seventy-two."

Mr. Jacobi gives me a little bit of a disgusted look, like, *Wow, if I'd gotten that grade, I wouldn't want it recorded either,* and then moves on. Mr. Jacobi is definitely not my biggest fan. It's mostly because I just cannot seem to get a handle on the quadratic formula. And that isn't even really my fault. My dad said that the quadratic formula is superhard, and he never learned it until ninth grade. And I'm only in seventh. Which seems really unfair. They're just moving formulas up, like, two whole grade levels.

The bell rings then, and I sigh and gather up my new math binder. I bought it last night in an effort to get myself more interested in math. It's this sparkly aqua color, and it has a place to put pics of you and all your friends on the inside. Of course, I haven't gotten around to that part yet.

I glance out of the corner of my eye at Little Miss Gymnast. She's sitting over on the windowsill now, stretching out her legs. I wonder why she's still doing that, when she's obviously dead. I mean, once you're a ghost, you really don't have to worry about your body anymore. But since she's a beautiful teenager, she probably won't believe me when I tell her that. Sigh.

At least she knows she's dead. That's one of the good things about seeing ghosts. I don't ever have to tell them they're dead. They already know, which is good, because can you imagine? It would be super-horrible if I had to tell them.

I let out another big sigh, and it must be a lot louder than I thought, because Brandon Dunham turns around and says, "I wouldn't worry about it, Kendall. It's just a quiz. You can make it up."

I guess he thinks I'm upset about my grade. Brandon Dunham knows all about my math grades. Mr. Jacobi makes us pass our quizzes to the person in front of us to grade, and Brandon sits in front of me. Which is really not fair. To make it even worse, then Mr. Jacobi goes around the room and you have to say your grade out loud so that he can record it. So the whole class knows how bad you did, which is *really* not fair.

"Yeah," I say. "I'm sure I can make it up." Sometimes Brandon and I talk. You know, just about little things, like we're doing now. I've been trying to work out how I can push us into we're-friends-and-talk-about-other-things-besides-school territory, but, like the quadratic formula, I haven't quite figured that out yet.

"You can," Brandon says. "I know once you get the hang of this stuff, you'll be able to do it in no time."

Hmmph. Easy for him to say. Brandon is, like, a math genius or something. He always gets 98 on his quizzes. I know this because of the whole saying-our-grades-out-loud thing.

And then I have it. The most perfect, brilliant idea ever.

"I don't know," I say, looking down at my binder and hoping I sound forlorn. "It's getting a little late in the year for me to be able to catch up."

Brandon looks confused. "It's only October."

"Yeah, well, it's never too early to start thinking about your future." This is a very smart thing to say. My dad always says it, and he's pretty much the smartest person I know. Of course, whenever *he* says it, I always just blow it off, because who really listens when their parents say something like that? But I can still appreciate the smartness of it.

"I guess." Brandon turns around to leave, and I see him slipping out of my grasp, like a slippery little fish.

"I wish," I say really loud and pointedly, "that I had someone to tutor me."

"They have an after-school tutoring program," Brandon says. "They meet every Wednesday after school. It's down in the math lab."

"Thanks," I say. "I'll definitely look into that. But it's too bad that we have another quiz tomorrow. You know, before I'll have a chance to get to the math lab."

"We have another quiz tomorrow?" Brandon starts leafing through his planner. It's a lie, of course. We don't have another quiz tomorrow, but can't the guy get the hint that I want him to tutor me? I mean, seriously. My dad says I'm about as subtle as a Mack truck. So either Brandon is really dense or I'm not doing a good job of getting my point across.

"Well, no," I say, because I realize that if he thinks we're going to have a quiz and we don't, he'll know I lied. "I just have a lot of anxiety about quizzes, so I tell myself that we have them every day. You know, so I'll make sure to study." Brandon nods, like this makes perfect sense to him. "Plus I'm going to ask Mr. Jacobi if I can do a makeup quiz tomorrow. To erase my grade. But only if I can study a lot tonight."

This whole time the blond gymnast in the corner has been watching with fascination. She probably thinks I'm crazy. I bet she always had, like, three bazillion boys asking her out all the time, and used to date the hottest guy in school. But I don't care if she's watching. Ghosts don't really make me self-conscious. I mean, how can they? They're dead. No matter how amazing they used to be, I still have one thing over them: I'm alive.

"You can do it," Brandon says. He shoots me his amazing smile. He has the most amazing perfectly straight white teeth. And his eyes twinkle. Seriously. His eyes twinkle when he smiles. Like a prince in a Disney cartoon or something.

He turns to go, and I sigh yet again.

"Oh, for God's sake," Blond Gymnast says, vaulting off the windowsill in one smooth movement. "If you want to study with him, then just ASK HIM." I cock my head and give her an incredulous look. "Do it!" she says. I give her an even more incredulous look. "Boys are dumb," she says. "He doesn't get it."

He doesn't? That seems a little unlikely, since I was practically throwing myself at him. But I guess she could be right. I definitely buy into the whole boys-are-dumb thing, and this girl seems like the kind of person who would know about stuff like this.

"Hey!" I yell at Brandon's back, right as he's about to

walk out of the classroom. "Do you want to study together? Today? After school? In the library?" Blond Gymnast rolls her eyes, I guess because she knows that I'm making a big mess out of asking him. But what does she want from me? It's a miracle I even asked him in the first place.

"Sure," Brandon says. "I'll meet you after eighth. Is it okay if Kyle comes?"

"Of course," I say, my heart soaring.

"Finally!" Blond Gymnast says, once Brandon's out the door of the classroom. "Now we can get to my problem. Which is way worse than some middle school study date." Right. There's that. And figuring out who Kyle is.

I've been able to see ghosts pretty much as long as I can remember. My mom left me and my dad when I was just a few months old, and so at first my dad thought I was making up all these imaginary friends because I was looking for a mother figure.

He thought I'd grow out of it, but I didn't, and right around the time I turned eight, I figured it probably wasn't the best idea to bring it up anymore. My dad was totally overwhelmed with everything he had going on—raising a daughter all by himself, keeping up our house, and working super-long hours trying to get his contracting business off the ground. So I decided it was best to stop talking about it, since he was starting to act all worried every time

I brought it up. I realized it was pretty abnormal to see ghosts, and so I haven't told anyone since.

I'm not sure exactly when I figured out that if I help the ghosts, they leave. It's kind of like asking someone when they realized that they loved their parents, or that they liked chocolate. It was just . . . there. Obviously I couldn't help the ghosts when I was younger. I just saw them kind of milling about. They'd come and hang out with me when they were bored, or needed someone to talk at. It seemed like they enjoyed seeing me as a baby and as a little kid, I guess because it reminded them of the circle of life or whatever.

Anyway, I'm much older now—twelve, almost thirteen, and in seventh grade—so obviously I'm in a much better position to help people. Although you'd be surprised at how many ghosts get annoyed when they realize I'm the one who's going to give them what they need to move into the afterlife. They pitch fits about me being so young. Can you imagine? It's like, beggars can't be choosers, you know? And I'm really good at what I do. I've never met a ghost that I couldn't help.

Still, I try not to get too upset with them if they get cranky. They are dead, after all.

Anyway, it becomes pretty obvious that Blond Gymnast is going to be the kind of ghost that tries my patience, because as we head out of math, she starts to freak out.

"Hello!" she's shrieking as we walk down the hall to my next class. "Are you going to help me or what?"

Sometimes the best thing to do with ghosts is just ignore them until they realize that shouting and stuff won't get them anywhere. They also need to understand that I have to work with them on my own time. You know, when I'm alone and can talk to them without people thinking I'm crazy. Usually they get the message pretty quickly, but not this time. Blond Gymnast is pushy.

"I know you have *sooo* much to think about," she says, all snotty, "with your little study date and all, but this is important. Life-and-death stuff."

I seriously doubt that, because she's already dead. So it can't *really* be a matter of life and death. Unless she's talking metaphorically, which I guess she could be. Even though she probably doesn't even know the meaning of the word "metaphorical." I laugh to myself, but this makes Blond Gymnast angry. "Hello!" she shrieks again. "Over here, Lady Gaga!"

I gasp. I know exactly why she's calling me Lady Gaga. Lady Gaga is known for her crazy sense of fashion and hairstyles. And today I'm sporting my hair in a very cute style of three tiny braids to the side, then pushed back off my face and held with three tiny glitter clips. I like to do my hair to match my mood, and this morning I was feeling very whimsical. It's all I can do not to dignify this with a response, and I just keep marching to French class.

"Fine!" she says, throwing her hands up in the air. "For some reason you are pretending not to hear me." Um, maybe because if I talk to you, people will think I'm crazy? "I'll meet you after school. In the library."

Great. Looks like my date with Brandon is now going to be a double.

Chapter

2

In French I pull out my cell and text my best friend, Ellie. I decide to do the text in the French language, because I promised my dad that I wouldn't text during class. Technically we're not even supposed to have cell phones in school, and I've already gotten detention for it once. But I figure that if I'm texting in the language I'm supposed to be learning, it's okay. Like bringing what you learn in the classroom to your real-world experience.

ME: *Bonjour mon amie!*

ELLIE: *Stop txting in French! I take Spanish. No clue what u r saying.*

ME: *Je suis desolee!*

ELLIE: *Bye.*

ME: *No, jk jk jk! 911 emerg! Have somehow asked Brandon Dunham to study w me after school!*

ELLIE: *Nooooo!*

ME: *Ouiii!!!!* Even Ellie knows that one.

ELLIE: *Kendall!!!!!!!*

ME: *Just 1 thing—do u know who Kyle is?*

ELLIE: *Kyle = Brandon's new BFF! Semi-new kid. V. cute!*

I rack my brains and have a faint memory of a Justin Bieber–haired boy being introduced to us in my earth science class.

ME: *He is coming too* ☹.

ELLIE: *I heart him, omg.*

ME: *U heart kyle?*

ELLIE: *Oui!!*

ME: *Wanna come?*

ELLIE: *Yes, perf! Double date!*

ME: *Yay! Adios, senorita! Ly xxxo.*

My double-date gymnast friend just got bounced for Ellie. Although, something tells me she'll still find a way to show up.

"How does my hair look?" I ask Blond Gymnast. It's eighth period, when I have independent study. (Our school's fancy way of saying "study hall." It's a total waste of time, since I never do my homework because I'm usually too amped up from the day and/or the anticipation of going home.) I'm in the English office. My English teacher, Mrs. D'Amico, lets me hang out in here during my free periods.

There's a big, cozy chair in the corner with a red glittery slipcover that I brought in myself, and one of those super-fancy coffeepots that make one cup of coffee at a time. I'm not really supposed to be using it, but Mrs. D'Amico doesn't care. She's, like, seventy-five and was BFF with my grandma before my grandma died two years ago, so she's known me since I was little.

"Listen," Blond Gymnast says, ignoring my question about how my hair looks and grabbing me by the shoulders. "This is important."

I walk over to the corner and start getting ready to mix up a mocha latte. I'm a caffeine addict.

"It's always very important," I say, sighing. While the machine roars to life, I pull a notebook out of my bag. I'm a very big fan of notebooks. I have a bunch of different colors for different things. My pink one is for possible book ideas, so that I can write them all when I grow up and become a famous writer. My green one is for pasting or drawing in pictures of hairstyles that I've seen in different maga-zines and/or have come up with in my head. My blue one is my journal (although I'm never completely honest when I write in it, because I'm always afraid I'm going to lose it and someone will read all my secrets). And my red one is where I keep all my notes for different ghost problems.

I open to a crisp page in the red one, then curl up in the chair and wait for Blond Gymnast to get started.

"It's Jen," she says. "You need to—"

Then she closes her mouth.

"Yes?" I ask, sighing. "I have to what?" I grab my latte from the beeping machine. Yum. Just the right amount of everything. I reach under the chair for my special shaker of cinnamon and shake a little bit on top of my drink.

"I . . . I . . . I don't know," she says. And then she stamps her foot. "I don't remember! All I know is that you have to find Jen!"

"*Find Jen*" I write in my notebook. "And you?" I say to her. "Do you have a name?" I might as well know who she is if I'm going to become all intimately involved in her life.

"Of course I have a name," she says. She vaults up onto Mrs. D'Amico's desk and onto a big pile of papers. She really likes sitting on things, this girl. "I'm Daniella."

"Nice to meet you, Daniella," I say. Not.

"So how does this work?" she says. "You find Jen, and then I get to, what, go to heaven or something?"

"Not really," I say. I set my latte on the little table next to my chair and start pulling the braids out of my hair. They're super-cute, but I don't think they're appropriate for a study date. I need to go for something a little more . . . flirty. French braid? No, too serious. Swingy ponytail? No, too sporty. Hmmm. I wish I'd brought my curling iron to school. I keep asking my dad for one of those cute little battery-powered ones that you can bring everywhere, but he's says it's an unnecessary expense. I think he's afraid I'll spend all my time doing my hair and never get to class on time.

"Then how does it work?" Daniella demands.

"You have to tell me who this Jen person is, where she is, what you want me to tell her, that sort of thing. Then I do it and you move on." I shrug. "To where, I have no idea."

"But—"

The door to the English office opens, and Mr. Jacobi is standing there. "Hi, Mr. Jacobi," I say happily.

"Kendall!" he says. "What are you doing in here?" He looks around suspiciously, like maybe I'm trying to change my grade or something, which is ridiculous, since English is my best subject.

"Just studying." I wave the red notebook in his face.

"Well," he says, "it's highly inappropriate, you being in here. Mrs. D'Amico would—"

"Mrs. D'Amico said I could," I tell him. "I've been doing it since the beginning of the year. What are you doing here?" I ask. "I didn't know math teachers were allowed to hang out in the English office."

"He's cute," Daniella says, walking toward Mr. Jacobi. "In one of those weird hipster kind of ways." She's looking

15

at him. "Although, he should really shave. Scruffiness is so last year." She wrinkles her nose at Mr. Jacobi's apparent lack of fashion sense.

"Math teachers are allowed to hang out wherever they want," Mr. Jacobi says, looking all indignant. "And not that it's any of your business, but I had a question for Mrs. D'Amico about next month's assembly."

"He's crushing on Mrs. D'Amico!" Daniella says. I resist the urge to roll my eyes. Mrs. D'Amico is seventy-five.

The bell rings then, and I gather up my stuff. "Time to go!" I say to Mr. Jacobi. "And don't worry about my quiz grade. Brandon and I are going to stay after school and study."

I check my watch on the way out of the office. Perfect. Just enough time to head to the girls' bathroom and fix my hair into something tousled and flirty and cute. I turn around and look down the hall to see if Daniella's following me. But she's gone.

My trip to the bathroom turns out to be a complete and total disaster, so I have to go looking for Ellie. When I finally find her at her locker, I fling myself toward her and scream, "My hair is a disaster!"

She sighs and grabs her book bag. "Your hair," she says, "is not a disaster."

"Come," I say. I drag her into the bathroom, where I

reach into my bag and pull out my special butterfly clips. "Start putting these all over my hair," I say. I flip open my green notebook and point to a page. "Like that girl."

"Oooh, cute," Ellie says. She starts clipping them all up and down my hair. That's one of the things I love about Ellie. She gets that I need a different hairstyle for my different moods. "I love these clips."

"Made them myself," I say proudly. "Butterfly rings, ten for a dollar, so I bought a bunch, ripped off the ring part, and then hot-glued them onto a clip."

"Brill!"

"Thanks."

"So it turns out I really like Kyle," Ellie says after a few minutes of clipping. "I just decided last period."

"Wow," I say. "How'd you come to that conclusion?" I'm not rattled by this news. Ellie crushes on a different boy pretty much every week, so the fact that she's decided to like Kyle isn't really that noteworthy, since by Friday she'll probably like someone else.

"Well, I remembered this one time when I overheard him saying that he liked watching that show *Scandals and Secrets*? And you know that's my fave show. Also, I like the way he's always eating licorice." She blushes.

"You already know his fave show and that he likes to eat licorice? Hasn't he only been here for, like, a month?"

"Yes," she says, and her blush deepens. "Also, he keeps

a picture of his dog taped to the inside of his math book. Which is adorable."

"The dog's adorable? Or the fact that he keeps a picture of it?"

"Both."

I study my reflection in the mirror. My long light brown hair looks wavy and cute, and the butterfly clips glitter and sparkle under the bathroom lights. "I'm ready."

"Are you going to really work on your math?" Ellie asks as we walk toward the library.

"Of course!" I say. "That's the only reason Brandon agreed to hang out with me."

Ellie nods, but she looks kind of disappointed. She probably wanted to do something a lot more fun. Ellie is one of those people who never has to study but still gets good grades. It's totally unfair, but she never brags about it. "How come you never asked me to tutor you?" she asks.

"I don't know," I say. "I guess I hoped I'd be caught up by now." We're standing in front of the library, and we walk in, whooshing through the turnstiles.

"They're over there," Ellie says, pointing to the corner, where Brandon and Kyle are sitting, books strewn about in front of them.

"Okay," I say, more to myself than to Ellie. "Now, be cool."

"Hey," Kyle says as we approach. "We thought it would

be more fun to study at the mall. You girls in?" He slams his book shut and slides it into his bag.

It's such an absurd thing to say that at first I think he has to be joking. "Study at the mall? Ha!" I almost add, "Kyle, you're such a kidder," but decide that would be going too far, since I hardly know him.

"Seriously," Kyle says. "They have free Wi-Fi in the food court, and we can get smoothies and spread out our stuff. It doesn't get busy there until, like, six." He pulls a piece of licorice out of his bag and pops it into his mouth, then pulls out another piece and offers it to Ellie.

"Thanks," she says shyly, and takes it. Kyle smiles at her. He has a very nice smile. I turn to Ellie, waiting for her to back me up about this whole mall thing. But instead she takes a bite of licorice, then turns to me and says, "What do you think?"

"I think it's crazy," I say. "I mean, how are we even going to get to the mall? Unless one of us turned sixteen since sixth period, I'd assume that none of us can drive yet." I laugh again, hoping they'll all see how completely ridiculous they're being. I mean, I love the mall, but I don't love getting in trouble.

"We take the city bus," Kyle says. "It picks us up right outside of school, and it drops us off at the front entrance of the mall." He sounds like he thinks it's crazy that I don't know this. Which kind of makes sense, because you'd think

19

that a girl my age who's so into accessories would know the bus routes to the mall.

"What do you think?" Ellie asks again. Which isn't that cool, since she's kind of leaving it up to me to say no. The thing about Ellie is that even though she can be shy, she's also pretty adventurous. She likes to be out and about, doing things. And since she didn't really need to study in the first place, going to the mall probably sounds super-fun to her.

"Sure," I say, even though what I really think is that if my dad finds out, he's going to kill me. Taking the bus to the mall? He definitely wouldn't be pleased. Although . . . he *is* always encouraging me to hang out after school and make new friends. He gets worried sometimes that I rely on Ellie too much. Of course, if he knew I was going with boys, he probably wouldn't be happy, but friends are friends, right? To be concerned about the gender of my friends would be pretty sexist.

"Cool," Kyle says, and before I know it, we're out of the library and on the street.

Chapter

3

"**Are you sure this** is okay?" Ellie asks once we're outside and the boys are a few feet ahead of us. Okay, more than a few feet. More like a hundred feet or so. Which doesn't make sense for a couple of reasons, one of which is that they said the bus stop was right outside the school, which obviously isn't true, and the other is that we're supposed to be together. So why are they walking so far ahead of us?

"Not really," I say. I texted my dad earlier to tell him I was staying after school to study. And I guess I didn't *specifically* say I'd be in the library, but still. I don't like lying to my dad. My dad is very cool.

"Should we call it off?" Ellie bites her lip and looks nervous.

"Bus!" Kyle screams from up ahead as a big blue and white bus comes whipping around the corner.

The boys start running, and Brandon turns around to yell, "Come on!" but neither one of them comes back for us. My heart sinks, because I was hoping Brandon was the type who'd be chivalrous and walk with me. Or at least act like he cared if I got on the bus.

Ellie and I look at each other, and then we start running, which really sucks because I hate running and also because the bus has to stop and wait, and when we finally get on, everyone's looking at us. The bus is full of people, and you can tell they're annoyed that we've held them up for even one second.

I plop into a seat next to Brandon, suddenly feeling very, very cranky.

"Sorry about that," he says. "The next one doesn't come for another forty-five minutes, and I thought I should go ahead so that I could hold it for you guys." He reaches into his pocket and hands me his gloves. "Here," he says. "It's cold out."

It *is* unseasonably cold for October, but suddenly I feel very hot. Still . . . I want to wear those gloves. Badly. So I slip my fingers in and wiggle them around. The gloves are too big for me, but somehow they feel right. Yay! Brandon is chivalrous after all!

"Thanks," I say, acting like it's no big deal and that I wear boys' gloves all the time.

I look over to where Ellie is sitting across from us, next to Kyle. She's got a very calm look on her face as she watches the whole thing with the gloves, which is a giveaway that she's freaking out inside. Ellie is very good at hiding her emotions.

The mall is actually pretty close to our school, but just far away enough not to be within walking distance, so we're there in what seems like two minutes. I haven't even gotten the chance to say anything to Brandon. Seriously, nothing.

We've just both been sitting here, not saying anything. It's kind of awkward, honestly, but the longer the silence goes on, the harder it is to break. It's like I need to come up with the perfect thing to say to him, and when I can't, I can't say anything. I mean, who wants to break the silence with some ridiculous comment?

God, I really do not know how to flirt. It's probably because I don't have a mom. Aren't moms supposed to teach you how to flirt? Or are they supposed to not want you to flirt because it means you're growing up too soon and all that other stuff that parents get all freaked out about?

The bus opens its doors and spits us out right onto the sidewalk in front of the mall.

"I want to get a new hat," Kyle says. He hands Ellie another piece of licorice without even asking if she wants it. Apparently those two are already so cozy that they're sharing food like it's nothing.

"What kind of hat?" Ellie asks.

"Baseball."

"Yeah, but what team?"

"Yanks."

Ellie wrinkles up her nose. "The Sox are so much better this year." Ellie knows all about sports. You'd think I would too, since I live with my dad, but who has time for sports with all these ghosts bothering me? Honestly, that's one of the reasons I've never gotten involved in any extracurriculars. No time. That's definitely going to have to change when I get into high school, though. How am I going to get into a good college with no after-school activities?

"Let's sit here!" I say, pointing to an empty table in the middle of the food court. It's right near a Coffee Bean, which is fab. I need a pick-me-up.

"First we need to get my hat," Kyle says.

I sigh. How is shopping for a hat with Kyle going to get me closer to Brandon? But I obviously can't say that, and so we all traipse into Lids.

"Yo, these hats are penny," Kyle says, looking them over.

I have no idea what "penny" means, but I try to stay in the spirit of things. I pick up a pink knitted Bruins hat and pull it down onto my head. Very cute. I could totally style my hair around this in a bunch of different ways. I pull it off and check the price tag, trying not to think about how many other people tried it on before me. It's $29.95? Wow.

That's a little bit ridiculous. I put it back on the shelf. I can probably find the same one at Target for five dollars.

"You should get that," a voice says, and I jump. Daniella. Right there, in the hat store with me.

"Go away," I whisper. "Can't you see I'm on a date?"

"You think this is a *date*?" she says. "This is not a date, unless you call being pulled along on Kyle's shopping trip a date."

I look around. Kyle is wrapping a tape measure around his head and saying, "I need to know my hat size. It can't be too small or too big, I don't want to have to bring this hat back!" The salesgirl is looking at him warily, and then Kyle whips the tape measure off his head and starts flailing it all around like it's a lasso.

Ellie is looking at him with disdain, and I already know what that means. She's over her crush. Brandon is in the corner, looking at a rack of key chains.

"It *is* a date," I say to Daniella, "and I can't be bothered with you right now, so if you want me to help you, come back later." I don't want to sound mean, but the last thing I want is for Daniella to start messing with my love life. She obviously doesn't care, though, because she follows me.

"Don't be so scared of Brandon," she says. "He's just a boy."

"I'm not scared of him!" I say. She looks at me skeptically. So to prove it I march right over to Brandon. I tap

25

him on the shoulder. "Hey," I say when he turns around, "want to go wait in the food court?" As soon as the words are out of my mouth, I want to take them back. That was *wayyy* too forward, especially for a girl like me who doesn't know how to flirt. I mean, I asked him to study. That was a miracle in and of itself.

"Uh, sure," he says, looking flustered. He puts the key chain he's holding back on the rack, and I turn around and mouth to Ellie, "OMG!" She just smiles and waves me away.

When we get to the food court, Brandon and I sit down at a big round table and spread out our books.

"Um, do you want a coffee or a soda or something?" I ask. "I'm going to go up to the coffee cart."

"I'm good," he says, pulling a Gatorade out of his bag.

I order my coffee, and when I get back to the table, Brandon has opened our books to the page our homework's on. I check my watch. Three fifteen. I have to get back to the school by five thirty, since that's when my dad is picking me up.

"When's the next bus back?" I ask Brandon, trying to sound all casual, like I'm the type of girl who just takes off to the mall without letting her dad know and doesn't freak out about it.

"Bus back to where?"

"School."

"I don't know." He shrugs. "Usually our parents just pick us up here."

"Oh." I try not to start hyperventilating.

Daniella, who was suspiciously absent while I was getting my coffee, is suddenly sitting next to me. "You are so in trouble," she says. "How are you going to get back to the school by five thirty? Your dad is going to be *sooo* mad."

She doesn't even know my dad, so obviously she's just saying it to make me freak out. And it must show on my face, because Brandon says, "Do you need a ride home?"

"No," I say. "It's not a big deal. My dad was going to pick me up at school, but I can just call him and tell him to pick me up here instead." Not.

"You'll probably get grounded," Daniella says cheerfully. She's on the floor now, doing a split. What a show-off!

"It's no problem," Brandon says. "My dad can bring you home. You live near the Windsor Cemetery, right?"

"Yeah," I say. "Right in front of it, actually. How'd you know?"

"Um, I've been to the cemetery a lot," he says, looking embarrassed. "Sometimes I see you outside with your dad."

"You have a cemetery in your front yard?" Daniella says. "Well, that explains a lot."

I want to tell her that no, it doesn't. I have no idea if the cemetery even means anything. My dad lives in the same house I do, has for even longer than I have, and he can't see ghosts. Well, as far as I know, anyway.

"So," I say to Brandon. "Should we get started?" I figure if we do a little studying, I won't technically be lying to my dad. At least, not that much. But what I really want to do is ask Brandon why he's always at the cemetery. I'm pretty sure that would be prying, though. It *is* only our first date. We'll have plenty of time to get into serious conversations later.

"Sure," Brandon says. "Just let me text my dad and let him know you need a ride."

But before we can even open a book, something totally horrible happens. Well, two things, actually. First Daniella starts screaming. I mean, she has a screechy voice anyway, but this is, like, a whole other level.

"Who," she shrieks, "is *that*?"

I follow her gaze over to the other side of the food court, where a teenage boy is holding hands with a girl with short red hair. I don't say anything. I can't, since (a) Brandon's right there, and (b) I have no clue who those people are. So Daniella just keeps on ranting. "I'll tell you who that is," she says. "*That* is Trevor Santini. But who that *girl* is, I don't know."

I may be clueless when it comes to boys, but I know enough to realize that Daniella must have liked this Trevor Santini person. Although, I can't see why. He's eating a big steak-and-cheese sandwich, and cheese is dripping all over his mouth, and a string of it even gets onto his shirt and makes a big grease stain. How disgusting.

But before I can worry about Trevor and Daniella, the second horrible thing happens—a voice comes booming across the food court. "Kendall Nicole Williams!"

I look up. Oh. My. God. My dad is here! My dad is at the mall, in the food court, and he's marching over to where I'm sitting. He looks so mad that he might explode.

I pretend I don't see him, then quickly pull my phone out and type him a quick text. *Going to study at the mall— getting a ride home w Brandon. c u soon!* Then I press send.

"Um, is that your dad?" Brandon asks as my dad comes weaving through the tables.

I wonder if I can say no, but since my dad has already spotted me and is making a beeline for our table, I decide to take another tack.

"Oh, hi, Dad!" I say brightly. "Did you get my text? Did you come to visit me?"

My dad ignores me and peers down at Brandon. "Who are you?" he demands.

"I'm Brandon Dunham, sir," Brandon says, standing up and holding his hand out. "I'm a friend of Kendall's from school. It's nice to meet you."

My dad looks at Brandon's hand suspiciously, but then finally reaches out and shakes it. "Ellie's here too," I say, so that my dad doesn't think Brandon and I are on some kind of date. (Even though we are.)

Next to me Daniella snorts, and I shoot her a dirty look.

"See!" I say, pointing over to the side of the food court, where Ellie's walking over to us, Kyle trailing a little way behind her. "There she is! Ellie! Ellie, we're over here!" It's only when she gets a little closer that I realize she's holding hands with Kyle. What? Why? I thought she was over him once he used that tape measure as a lasso.

"Wow," Daniella says. "Your friend is a fast mover." But the drama I'm having must not really excite her that much, because before I can throw her another dirty look, she's wandered over to where Travis Santini is sitting. He's holding hands with the red-haired girl and looking into her eyes like he's totally lovesick. Something tells me that's really going to make Daniella mad.

Ellie waves at me with her free hand, but when she sees my dad, she frowns, then gets a panic-stricken look on her face.

"Well!" my dad says, his gaze falling on Ellie's and Kyle's intertwined hands. "I see you're on a double date!"

"No!" I say. "No, we're not on a double date!"

"Hi, Mr. Williams," Ellie says, walking up to the table. She's not holding Kyle's hand anymore, which is good, but also kind of too late since my dad already saw her. "What are you doing here?"

"Yeah, Dad," I say. "What are you doing here? Shouldn't you be at work?"

"I should be, yes," he says. "But then I got a call from Cindy Pollack, and she told me that she saw my daughter at the mall, hanging out in the hat store with boys. She thought it was just adorable that my daughter was on a date." He looks at Brandon suspiciously. "And I said, 'That's impossible. Kendall stayed after school to study in the library.' And then *she* said—"

"I get it, Dad," I say, interrupting him. "But you didn't have to leave work. You could have just called me."

"Luckily, I was working nearby," he says. "And I did try to call you." I reach down and look at my phone. Seven missed calls, all from my dad. I guess I couldn't hear my phone with all that loud music in the hat shop, not to mention Daniella freaking out. I look over to where Travis Santini is sitting. Daniella's in one of the empty chairs at their table, gesturing wildly and yelling at the red-haired girl.

"Well, I texted you," I tell my dad. "But I guess you didn't get it! Anyway, now that you're here, maybe you could do some shopping, and then we can get dinner or something later." I figure this will definitely get him to calm down, because my dad loves the kung pao chicken they have in the food court. He's not really supposed to have it because of his cholesterol, but I think today we can make an exception.

31

"Kendall," my dad says, his tone icy. "I think it's best if we leave now."

Ellie looks down at the ground. Brandon looks superscared, which is understandable, since my dad *is* really scary. He's six foot two and has a beard, and he works construction, so he's always wearing Carhartt jackets and work boots. Even Kyle knows enough to keep his mouth shut.

So what else can I do? I gather up my books and follow my dad out the door. The only good thing is that Daniella doesn't follow.

Chapter

4

Okay, so that was really embarrassing. To have my dad walk in and *pull me* out of the mall like that? I'll never live it down. Not to mention the fact that I have to hear it all the way home in my dad's truck. ("I trusted you, Kendall. I can't believe you would go behind my back like that, Kendall." Blah, blah, blah, blah.)

Cindy Pollack is such a tattletale. Cindy Pollack, btw, is this very annoying blond woman who's friends with my dad. They went to high school together, and now she lives down the street from us. I keep trying to tell my dad that she wants to be more than friends with him, but he's totally in denial.

Anyway, by the time we get home, my dad has calmed

down a little bit. In fact, I think he feels kind of bad that he embarrassed me in front of my friends, because he doesn't say anything about me being grounded or anything. He just makes me promise that next time I'll let him know where I'm going to be.

Promise made, I run up to my room, pull on a comfy sweatshirt, and then grab my red notebook out of my bag and head over to the cemetery across the street.

The cemetery is where I go to think, to write, to hang out. I know spending time in a cemetery probably seems weird, and I guess it is, a little. But the cemetery is quiet and calm, and it's where my grandma is buried. She was the closest person to me until she died a couple of years ago, and there's a wooden bench right near her grave. I swear, when I'm there, it's like her spirit is calming me or something. Weird, right?

I settle in on my favorite bench, and then, all of a sudden, there's Daniella.

"I come here because it's peaceful," I say to her. "And since you're here, that's ruining it. So go away."

She sighs. "Travis Santini has moved on," she says, all dramatic. She flings herself onto the bench in despair.

I roll my eyes. I mean, I get it that it sucks that she's dead and the guy she likes has moved on. But let's face it, Travis Santini is no prize.

My phone beeps with a text. Ellie. *OMG, R U GROUNDED?*

34

I quickly text back, *No—what happened? What did B say? And why were u holding hands w/K????*

"Did you hear me?" Daniella yells.

"Yes," I say. "Travis Santini has moved on."

"Don't you even *care*?"

"Travis Santini was your boyfriend?"

"Well, no," she says. "Not exactly. But he was about to be."

"About to be doesn't count," I say, then turn back to my phone.

"Yeah, well . . ." She trails off and looks into the distance. "All I know is that I have to find Jen. And tell her it's not her fault. And then I can move on." I don't say anything. "And you have to help me, right?"

I want to say no, because she's kind of a brat. But the problem is, if I don't help her, she's just going to hang around and become more and more agitated, like, every single second. I tried to ignore a ghost once last year, even going so far as to pretend I couldn't see or hear her, but it didn't work. I never got even a moment's peace, and the whole thing culminated with her screaming at me in the middle of the school-wide chorus concert, which totally distracted me and made me sing the wrong lyrics.

"Yes," I say, sighing. "I'll help you." And then I add, "Not like I have a choice." Just in case she thinks it's her sparkling personality or something that's making me change my mind.

I pull out my red notebook, placing my phone on the bench just in case Ellie texts me back. "So," I say. "Can you please tell me who this Jen person is?"

"I don't know," she says, and shrugs her delicate little shoulders. "I just know that she's very important."

"Okay," I say. "And do you know who you are?"

"I'm Daniella," she says, and then rolls her eyes. "I already told you that." She's giving me a look now like she can't believe I'm the one that's supposed to help her move on. I want to tell her beggars can't be choosers, but if I annoy her too much, she might not remember what I need her to tell me.

"I know," I say, smiling tightly. "And you obviously remember Travis Santini, but do you remember anything else about your life? Where you lived, when you died, your last name, that kind of thing?"

"Well." She chews on her lip. "It must have been recently, because Travis and I are about the same age."

"Right," I say. "And since you remember him, he must have something to do with your unfinished business."

"Travis Santini does?" She frowns. "But what about Jen?"

"Jen does too."

"What, though? And who is Jen?"

"Well, I don't know."

"What do you mean, you don't know?" she shrieks. "Aren't you supposed to know all this stuff?"

"No," I say. "Unfortunately, I have to figure it out." I look down at my notebook. One Travis Santini, a maybe boyfriend. One mysterious girl named Jen. And one ghost with an attitude. I sigh. *So* not how I wanted to be spending my October.

The next morning at school I'm really, really dreading seeing Brandon. What if he thinks I'm completely lame now that he saw my dad hauling me out of the mall? What if he realizes that no matter what, he could never get involved with me since my dad is obviously way too overprotective and might freak out on him? What if he thinks I'm a total immature baby who's not allowed to date? (Note to self: Ask my dad if I can date.) What if—

"I like Kyle again," Ellie says in homeroom.

"I didn't know you stopped liking him," I say. "I mean, I figured you had, because you always stop liking people. But then you guys were holding hands."

"I went off him for a second," she says. "In the hat store. I mean, did you see what he was doing with that tape measure?" She wrinkles up her nose like she can't believe someone would act that way. "But then, after you and Brandon left, he was being really funny and sweet. He kept sharing his licorice with me, and when he was checking out, he asked me if I wanted anything from Lids. And then, when the cashier gave him two dollars extra in change, he returned it."

Hmmm. Asking her if she wanted anything *is* kind of cute. But still. "Are you sure you like him again?"

"Positive," she says. "And I think he likes me, too."

"Well, obvi," I say. "You're fabulous." I look down and play with the edge of my notebook. "Um, so what did Brandon say?" Ellie never texted me back yesterday, leading me to believe that she doesn't want to tell me what Brandon said.

"Brandon?" She looks uncomfortable.

"Yes," I say, "and you better tell me the truth."

"*Weeeell*, to be honest, your dad made him kind of nervous."

Great. I knew I was going to have to do some damage control. Thank God I did my hair in two French braids this morning, with glitter threads all through them, and that I'm wearing a super-cute black skirt that I made sparkly with my glitter gun. "So what should I do?" I ask Ellie.

"Honestly?" she says. "I think you should act like nothing's wrong, just pretend like—"

But the rest of what she's saying gets all swallowed up by Daniella. She pops right up next to me, still in her gymnastics uniform, and looking as fresh as a daisy. "Did you figure it out yet?" she demands. "Because I'm not getting any younger."

I sigh. Seriously? Like I don't have enough to worry about. Especially since I *haven't* figured it out yet. Not Daniella, and apparently not my love life.

· · ·

Brandon's not in math (which drives me crazy, because hello, I look really cute today and need to make him realize how mature and independent I am, the kind of girl who's totally capable of making decisions without her dad being involved—not to mention I spent all morning psyching myself up to see him), and that kind of makes the rest of the day drag by.

When eighth-period study hall finally rolls around, I skip my usual trip to the English office and decide to go to the computer lab to do a little research on Daniella. I figure it will keep my mind off Brandon and the reason he wasn't in math. And besides, I do need to get started. Daniella's driving me crazy, following me all around. She's incapable of talking at a normal volume too. She's been screaming and screeching at me all day.

I sit down in the back of the library, making sure my computer screen is facing the wall. No way I want people to see what I'm doing. One time at the beginning of the year someone caught me googling "dead people Boston," and I had to pretend that Dead People was the name of a new band and that I was checking their tour dates.

"Daniella teenager dead Boston area," I type now. A bunch of results pop up, mostly about a girl named Daniella who died in 1990. Not what I'm looking for.

Think, Kendall, I tell myself. *What else do you know*

about her? Well, I know she's wearing a gymnastics outfit. And that might be a clue.

So this time I google "high school gymnast dead," and that's when it pops up. An article about the Milford High gymnastics team, who all died in a bus accident earlier this year. They were on their way to a meet in Connecticut when the bus driver lost control of the bus and it went sliding off the road. I really should have remembered that. I know it sounds morbid, but usually I keep up with all the dead people around town. I have to. It's, like, job training.

I quickly find the Milford High online yearbook and Google "Jen." Of course there are, like, three million of them. I look for a picture of the gymnastics team, but when I find one, it's too small and I can't read the names or see the faces very well. Sigh. It looks like I'm going to have to make a trip to the high school after school.

I have to lie to my dad again about where I'm going, but I can't really be blamed for that. I mean, what choice do I have? It's not like I can just say, "Oh, hi, Dad. I have to go to the high school because I have to find some girl named Jen, and by the way did I ever mention I can still see ghosts? No? Oh, well, I can. Later!"

Luckily, the high school's within walking distance, so I don't have to take the bus again. I play with the end of one of my braids as I walk over there and think about Brandon.

His smile. The way his hair glints in the sunlight. Well. Not that I've ever really seen his hair glint in the sunlight. But it does look like the kind of hair that totally would.

When I get to the high school, there are groups of kids milling around on the sidewalk and the lawn, dressed in cheerleader uniforms and soccer shorts. Great. So basically now I have to find a girl named Jen while knowing nothing about her, including her last name or what she looks like.

"Hey!" Daniella yells, popping up next to me. I scream and drop the notebook I'm holding. A couple of girls sitting on a bench near me turn to stare. "Oh my God," Daniella says. "This is my school! I remember it!" She looks at me in awe. "God, this is so weird."

"Yeah," I say grumpily, brushing my notebook off. "Any chance you also remember Jen's last name?"

She shrugs. Yeah. I didn't think so.

"So what are we doing here?" she asks. I fill her in on what I found out earlier, about her team and the accident. "Wow," she says, her eyes wild. "That's, like, so dramatic."

She stays quiet as I plow through the crowd and into the school. Once I'm inside, I follow the sound of sneakers squeaking, figuring that since Daniella was a gymnast, it's a safe bet that I can learn something if I go to the gym. There's a boys' basketball team in there practicing, but I barge right in.

"What are you doing?" Daniella asks. "You can't just go—"

"Yoo-hoo!" I yell. "Excuse me!"

Daniella starts flipping out. "Stop!" she shrieks. She tries to bat my hands, but she just goes floating right through me. It's kind of funny, actually. "Stop! You can't just go around and yell at boys' basketball practice!"

Actually, she's wrong. Completely wrong. I've been on enough of these spy missions to realize that you have to go in and start yelling and getting your hands dirty, otherwise you'll never get anything done. Also, it's always better to talk to boys when you need information. Girls get way too suspicious and start asking all kinds of questions.

True to form, a guy wanders off the court toward me. He's all sweaty and wearing a basketball uniform. Gross.

"Oh my God," Daniella says. "I remember him! That's Mitch Huntsman. Do not talk to him, Kendall! He's a total jerk."

"Hello!" I say to him. "You're Mitch, right?"

"Yeah." He looks at me. "How did you know that?"

"My sister goes here," I say. "And she has a crush on you." I lower my eyes to the ground, like it's some big secret I shouldn't be talking about.

"Who's your sister?"

"I'll tell you," I say. "But first I need some help."

He looks back over his shoulder to the basketball practice in progress, but the thought of my older sister liking him must be too much to resist, because he turns back to me. "What do you need help with?"

I feel almost bad that my sister is fake. "Well," I say, "I'm supposed to give a message to this girl named Jen. From, uh, my sister. But I forgot Jen's last name, and the only thing I know about her is that she's on the gymnastics team."

At least I'm hoping she is.

"You mean Jen Higgins," he says. "She should be across the hall in the other gym. They practice at the same time we do."

"Thanks!" I say. He's nice. Daniella's totally wrong about him.

"He's only being nice to you because he thinks your fake sister likes him," Daniella mumbles. "He's totally girl crazy."

"Hey," Mitch calls after me when I'm almost out of the gym. "Who's your sister?"

"Umm . . ." I rack my brains. "Ellie Wilimena!" Ellie's the closest thing I have to a sister, so it's not exactly a lie, right?"

"Ellie Wilimena," Mitch says thoughtfully. "I think she's in my math class."

"God, what a jerk!" Daniella gets all up in Mitch's face. "You were a jerk when I was alive, and you're still a jerk now. Jerk, jerk, jerk, jerk, jerk!" Wow. Talk about being judgmental and over the top.

"Later!" I call to Mitch. Daniella follows me out of the gym, but she's still muttering under her breath.

"What's so bad about him?" I ask. "He seemed nice to me."

"Nice?" she says. "You think he was nice? He's totally self-absorbed. He always wears tight shirts to show off his muscles."

"Maybe he's just proud of his body," I say, shrugging.

"Ugh," she says, looking me up and down. "I weep for the future."

"You know what?" I say. "I'm getting kind of bored of this. I think I'm going to go home now. I have a lot of math homework anyway, so . . ."

"No, no, no. I'm sorry." She bites her lip. "I know I'm being a brat. This is all just . . ." She looks around. "A little overwhelming."

"Whatever," I say. I'm at the other gym now, and I peek in. There are about ten or twelve girls, all in their gymnastics uniforms, flipping around. Wow. They are really flexible. Now I just have to figure out which one Jen is.

"Good job, Jen!" an older woman with curly hair, who I'm assuming is their coach, yells as a pretty girl with long blond hair goes tumbling down the mats.

"Oh my God," Daniella says. "It's Jen." She starts to say something else. But before she can, she disappears.

Whatever. I mean, I'm kind of used to that. Ghosts disappearing when they get all overwhelmed. It's like their brains can't handle it or something, and so instead of fainting like a normal person would do, they just kind of . . . fade away. It's actually better for her. That she's gone. And better for me, too, since now it'll be a lot quieter.

I have to hang around until practice gets out, which almost gives me a heart attack, because I need to get back to school so that I can take the late bus home, or else my dad will definitely ground me.

I sit on the floor outside the gym (which is actually surprisingly clean—the custodians at this school must be way better than the ones at my school, since the floors there are super-disgusting) and work on my homework until the practice lets out. When it finally does, I'm totally ready for Jen. Jenny? Should I call her Jen or Jenny? Probably just Jen. No need to get cute.

"Hey, Jen!" I yell as she walks by, her backpack bouncing against the back of her dark purple hoodie. She turns around and looks at me. I haven't really figured out what I'm going to say to her. Which is okay. I'm always better on the fly.

"Yeah?" she asks.

"I just . . . um, I'm a gymnast." As soon as the words are out of my mouth, I realize I shouldn't have said them. I mean, I know nothing about gymnastics. I mean, I'm not *totally* unprepared. I did some quick googling, so I know a few of the basic moves. And I've used some of the equipment, like the balance beam and uneven bars, during our gymnastics unit in gym class. But that's about it. "And I was wondering if you could give me some pointers? Some very basic ones," I add quickly. "I'm kind of just starting out, so nothing too, ah, technical." Hmmm. So much for being better on the fly.

"You're a gymnast?" she says, shaking her head. She sounds confused. Which makes sense. After all, I'm just accosting her outside of practice, telling her I'm a gymnast looking for pointers. Not to mention that I really don't look like a gymnast. I'm short, at least, like gymnasts are, so that's good. But I think they wear their hair in ponytails a lot. Or buns. How boring.

"I'm sorry. What is it you're asking?" Jen asks, still sounding confused. She looks over her shoulder, like she's late for something.

"Yeah," I say. "I'm, um, a gymnast. I used to go and watch your meets all the time. I really admired your teammate Daniella." I look down at the ground like I'm all sad about her dying, but I'm looking up at Jen from below lowered lashes so that I can see her reaction.

"You watched Daniella Hughes?" Jen asks. Her voice softens, and I know I have the right Jen. Her whole face looks like she's longing to have Daniella back. I think about Ellie, about what I would do if anything ever happened to her, and my heart catches in my throat. This is the difficult part about what I do. Dealing with the dead people is easy, because they're all fine. Happy, even. It's the people that are left behind that are the ones that are hard to talk to.

"Yes," I say. "She was amazing on the beam." I don't know if it's true or not, but I'm taking a guess, and also since I know hardly anything about gymnastics, this is the best I can come up with.

Jen just stares at me.

"Wanna walk together?" I ask, forcing my voice to sound all friendly and not like I'm going to pump her for info about Daniella. "I have to be back at the middle school to catch my late bus, but I would really just love to talk to you."

"I can't," she says, looking over her shoulder again. "Sorry, but I don't have my mom's car today and I'm about to miss my own late bus."

"Oh. Right." I force myself to sound really disappointed. She's afraid of missing her late bus? She's sixteen. I'm sure her dad isn't going to freak out if she comes home late, like mine would. "Sorry, I just . . . I really was hoping to get some pointers from someone I admire." I look down at the ground like I'm devastated, and then turn and start walking away.

My gamble pays off, because I hear her sigh, and then she yells after me, "Wait! Where do you live?"

"In Briarwood," I say, turning around.

"Well, you'd be on my late bus," she says. She bites her

lip and thinks about it. "I could probably get you on. The driver doesn't even know who's coming or going half the time."

I think about it. It's a risk, because if for some reason the driver doesn't let me on, I'll miss my middle school late bus, and then I'll be stranded. Of course, I guess I could always just walk back to the middle school and then call my dad and tell him I missed the bus. But I don't know if he'd believe that after the whole fiasco in the mall yesterday.

I hesitate, but then Daniella comes back. "Oh my God," she says, her voice full of sadness. "It's Jen."

And her face looks so sad and her eyes fill with tears. And so when Jen says, "What's it going to be?" I follow her out the door and toward the bus.

Chapter

5

Wow. The high school late bus is kind of crazy. I cannot believe that this is what I'm going to be dealing with in a couple of years. No one's even *pretending* to sit in their seats, they're talking super-loud, and there are three kids in the back that are bopping a soccer ball around with their *heads*. I'm really not surprised that Daniella's bus driver got into an accident if this is how the kids were behaving. Talk about distracting.

"So," Jen says once we're settled into a seat in the middle of the bus. Someone's iPod goes flying over my head, followed by the sound of a kid yelling, "RYYYAAAN! THAT WAS MY IPOD, AND IF YOU BROKE IT, YOU'RE GOING TO PAY!" I clutch my bag a little tighter against my chest. "What do you want to know about gymnastics?"

Right. Gymnastics. Crap. How am I going to figure out what the heck happened between her and Daniella if we're talking about *gymnastics*? More importantly, how am I going to talk about gymnastics when I hardly know anything about it?

"Well," I say slowly, "I used to come to your meets and watch Daniella. She was my favorite gymnast." I pull out of my bag the picture of their team that I printed off the internet. "I wanted to have her sign this, but I always chickened out before I could ask her. She was so good that it was just . . . It was intimidating."

God, Daniella would love this if she were here. Even though I've never actually even seen her do any gymnastics (except for the splits and stuff she does to show off), she seems like the type that would eat up every compliment. But she left again when we got on the bus. I think she was afraid to hear what Jen would say. I don't blame her. I'm kind of afraid of what Jen might say too, especially if it's going to be "You're a liar, and you don't know anything about gymnastics, so leave me alone, you psycho."

Jen takes the picture and runs her hand over the printed faces. "You shouldn't have been intimidated," she says. "Daniella would have signed it. She loved her fans."

"Yeah, I'll bet she did," I say without thinking. Jen looks at me funny, so I quickly add, "She just seemed like she would be really nice, you know? I looked up to her so much." Wow, I'm really laying it on thick. So thick that for a second I wonder if I've gone too far.

But Jen just nods and hands the picture back to me. "A lot of people did. Daniella was amazing. Did you see her at the Central Square meet?"

"Yes," I lie. "She was awesome."

Jen looks at me and frowns. "That was the meet where she fell off the beam and had to be taken to the hospital."

"Oh," I say, smacking my forehead like I just got confused for a second. "That's right! I'm always getting her meets mixed up, since I went to so many."

"Anyway," she continues, "Daniella was right back out there as soon as the doctor said it was okay. I would have been scared, but not her."

"She was daring," I say, nodding my head.

"She was," Jen says. She smiles, remembering. "So what was your favorite move she did on the beam?"

"Oh, I liked them all," I say. For some reason my voice cracks. I really should have done a little more research on gymnastics before I came here. But I was assuming Daniella would be around to feed me info. But I guess not.

"Yeah," Jen presses, "but which one was your favorite?"

The bus is getting closer to my house now, and so I start to panic. Not only haven't I gotten any good information, but somehow Jen is the one who's interrogating *me*. "I liked

51

her cartwheel," I try. Daniella was doing cartwheels the first time I saw her, so I'm hoping maybe it's, like, her signature move or something. Plus who can really mess up a cartwheel?

"Daniella's cartwheels on the beam were horrible," Jen says quietly. Oopsies. "And the beam was her weakest event."

"Yeah," I try, "but that's why I liked Daniella so much as a gymnast. She never gave up trying to make those cartwheels better."

The bus is getting closer to my stop, and I'm starting to lose it. I have to get back on track here. But something's telling me I need to back off talking about Daniella and abort this mission, fast. "So we never really got a chance to talk about your gymnastics goals," I say in an effort to change the subject. "Are you hoping to get a college scholarship?"

She turns to me, her green eyes cold. "Are you looking for gossip or something?"

My mouth flops open. "Gossip?"

"No, of course not," she says, sounding like she's talking more to herself than to me. "You're too young to know any of us, but maybe you have an older sister or someone who sent you?"

"No," I say, shaking my head. "I don't have an older sister. And I'm not looking for gossip. I don't know what you're—"

"Then why are you so interested in Daniella?" she asks. The bus is turning onto my street now, and I have about thirty seconds before I have to get off.

"I told you," I say. "I'm a fan of hers. I love gymnastics, and—"

"Oh, please," she says as the bus pulls to a stop at the corner near my house. "You don't know anything about gymnastics." She stands up, giving me an icy stare. "And I don't want you to bother me ever again." And then she gets up and moves to another seat. And I'm left to run up the aisle of the bus like a crazy person so that I don't miss my stop.

Wow. So that whole thing was a complete and total disaster. I mean, Jen was onto me! Who knew Daniella's friends would be so smart? Once I'm off the bus, I run up to my room, grab my red notebook, and then head over to the graveyard. I'm hoping I'll be able to come up with some new plan to help Daniella. Preferably without ever having to see Jen again.

I settle down on my fave bench, open to a fresh page, and write "*PLAN B*" in big letters across the top. Now I just need to come up with an actual plan B. I'm still racking my brains when Daniella shows up.

"Oh, fancy seeing you here," I say, kind of snotty. "Where the heck have you been? She was asking me all those stupid questions about gymnastics! You had to know she was going to do that!"

"I just . . . I couldn't stay," Daniella says, ignoring the fact that I'm yelling at her. "It was too hard." She shakes her head, and I almost feel sorry for her. I mean, Daniella actually looks upset, like she's going to cry or something. It's different than when she saw Travis Santini in the mall. That was more like something that made her mad, and this . . . this is like she feels bad for someone else. Maybe she's not as self-centered as I thought.

I quickly tell her about Jen accusing me of looking for gossip. "And now . . . ," I sigh, "I have to somehow figure out a way to get her to talk to me. Which isn't really going to be easy, since she thinks I'm a total crazy person."

"Well, Kendall, it *was* pretty crazy how you tried to track her down at school like that. And after practice! Everyone knows that no one comes to practices! It would have been better if you'd just gone to one of her meets or something."

I stare at her, incredulous. *Now* she's telling me this? "*Now* you're telling me this?" I ask, throwing my hands into the air. "You could have told me that before this whole thing happened! And by the way, if you're going to—" But I stop talking because Daniella's face has gotten all scrunchy, and she's wrinkling up her nose and staring off into space. "What?" I ask. "Are you remembering something?"

"Yes," she says, pulling at her hair. "I mean, kind of. I'm . . . I'm remembering . . . digging."

"Digging?"

"Yeah, digging."

"Digging, like in the dirt?"

"Yes." She looks at me and shakes her head. "And now it's gone."

"Great," I say. I slide off the bench and flop down in the grass near my grandma's headstone. I stare up at the sky, watching the clouds drift lazily with the breeze. "We are in so much freaking trouble."

Digging in the dirt? What kind of thing is that to remember? Why the heck would Daniella be digging? She's definitely not the outdoorsy type. Is it possible she's just remembering her own funeral? Maybe Jen didn't come to her funeral, and so Daniella's all mad about it? God, I hate this part. Trying to figure things out can be so frustrating!

A little boy and a woman go walking by, holding hands. The woman gives me a sympathetic look, I guess because she thinks I'm mourning whoever's grave I'm at. But even though I'm at my grandma's grave, and I do miss her more than anything, I'm not sad for her. I know she's moved on to somewhere better.

"What's she looking at?" Daniella asks, staring at the woman. "Move it, lady. Nothing to see here!" She waves her hand at her.

I laugh, and the woman gives me a disapproving look.

"Come on," I say to Daniella, sighing and picking myself up off the grass. "Let's get out of here."

When I get home, my dad's at the stove, stirring something really yummy-smelling in the frying pan. There's a cut-up pile of tomatoes and lettuce sitting on a platter on the counter.

"Hey, honey," he says. I peek into the frying pan.

"Mmmm, tacos," I say, inhaling the scent of ground beef and spices. "Delish."

"Tacos are so good," Daniella says. "I wish I could have some." Ghosts don't really ever get hungry. But they do sometimes crave food. It's like they can't break the emotional attachment they have. "Not that I ever ate them much when I was alive." She sighs. "I was always in training."

"Try this." My dad holds a spoon of seasoned ground beef out to me. "Does it need anything?"

"Yum," I say, eating it. "No, it's perfect."

"So how was studying after school?" he asks, turning back to the pan.

"Good," I say, feeling a little uncomfortable that I told my dad I was staying after again. But it's not like I did it to hang out with Brandon. I was on official business. I grab a handful of shredded cheese out of the bowl on the counter and pop it into my mouth. If my dad's suspicious about me staying after school, he doesn't say anything, which actually makes me feel worse. Obviously he still trusts me, even after what I did yesterday.

"Kendall," he says, "don't do that with the cheese."

"Why not?" I ask. "I washed my hands."

My phone vibrates. A text from Ellie. *Talked to Kyle abt u and Brandon! He is def into you, will call u tonight with deets!*

Tonight? Is she crazy? I cannot wait until *tonight* to get deets! I'm about to text her back that she better tell me now, before I freak out and completely die from anticipation, but then my dad says something that makes me forget all about Brandon.

"Cindy's coming to dinner."

"What? *Why?*"

"I ran into her at the grocery store, and she saw the taco ingredients in my cart, and she mentioned that Mexican is her favorite. So I invited her over."

"Who's Cindy?" Daniella says, looking interested. "Is she your dad's girlfriend?"

"Dad, she's not your girlfriend," I say. It's more for Daniella's benefit than anything else, but it's also good to remind my dad of this fact any chance I get. Then I glare at Daniella while my dad's back is turned. When she sees Cindy, she'll figure out the ridiculousness of even asking if Cindy is my dad's girlfriend. No one who meets Cindy Pollack would ever think that.

"I know that, Kendall," my dad says, pulling three plates down from the cabinet over the dishwasher. "But she *is* my friend, and I expect you to be nice to her while she's here."

"Of course I'll be nice to her," I grumble.

"Wow," Daniella says. "I guess you don't like this Cindy person too much. She's the one who told on you for being at the mall, right? What a jerk."

She's right. I don't like Cindy too much. Even though, I guess, technically, she didn't tell on me for being at the mall. I mean, according to my dad, she thought it was cute.

The thing about Cindy is that even though she's not my dad's girlfriend, she *wants* to be. Which is not okay. And not because I don't want my dad to have a girlfriend. It's just that I don't want him to have Cindy as a girlfriend. She's loud and opinionated, and every time she sees me, she says something like, "Ohmigod, Kendall, your hair looks so hip!"

She's trying to be nice, because she thinks we should be BFF. It's totally fake, of course—she just wants to get in good with me so that she can get closer to my dad. I mean, making a comment about my hair? Cindy knows nothing about hair. Hers is horrible, this bleach blond mess that she styles up so high, it looks like some kind of beehive with bangs.

Of course, my dad thinks I don't like Cindy because I don't want her dating him, and he thinks it has to do with my mom leaving when I was a baby. Which it so doesn't. I mean, of course I don't like the fact that my mom left when I was so young. But I do want my dad to be happy, and if that means dating, I'm totally fine with it. I just don't think he'd be happy with Cindy, and honestly, I don't think he does either, because if he did, he'd be dating her.

When the doorbell rings a couple of minutes later, I get really busy playing around with my phone, texting Ellie back.

"Kendall," my dad says, "can you go and answer the door, please?"

"Fine," I grumble, sighing like it's a big imposition, and then shuffling my feet all the way to the front door.

"Hello!" Cindy says when I open the door. She's wearing a low-cut black sweater and holding a store-bought cherry pie. "How are you, Kendall? I love your shirt. It's so retro hippy."

"Thanks." I look down at the shirt I'm wearing, a brand-new aqua T-shirt with a rainbow across the front. I had some cool rainbow beads that I wanted to put in my hair, and I thought it would be awesome if I had a shirt to match. But this shirt is definitely not retro.

Cindy follows me to the kitchen, and I suffer through dinner, not even able to enjoy my tacos as Cindy prattles on about things that are really boring, like tax rates and some new dining room table she's planning on buying.

"Can I be excused?" I ask finally as Cindy wraps up some really long story about a problem she's having with the guy she hired to renovate her kitchen.

"No," my dad says. "We haven't even had dessert yet."

"I'm full," I say, draining the last of my milk.

"I hope you're not mad that I called your dad when I saw you at the mall yesterday, Kendall," Cindy says. "I didn't know you were on a secret date." She looks at me and winks, like we're two old friends.

"It's fine," I lie. "I'm not mad." I grab a plain taco shell off the plate on the table, break off a bite, and pop it into my mouth, hoping she'll see that my mouth's full and so I can't talk. And what does she mean, "a secret date"? It wasn't a secret date. It was just some friends getting together to study.

"Wow," Daniella says. She's standing behind Cindy's chair, peering into her hair. "How does she get her hair to stay up so straight like that?"

"I don't know," I say.

"You don't know what?" my dad says.

"Nothing." I put my fork down. "Dad, please can I be excused? I have a lot of homework to do, and I don't really feel like dessert." I pat my stomach. "I'm full."

My dad hesitates, but then finally says, "Okay."

Cindy looks happy, like she can't wait to be alone with my dad. But I don't even care, because I'm too excited to be out of there, and even more excited to finally be able to call

Ellie and get the deets on what Brandon told Kyle.

"I knew you were going to call," Ellie says when she picks up. "You are, like, the most impatient person ever."

"That's so not true," I say, leaning back onto my bed and settling in for a nice long gossip session. My bed is perfect for long phone calls with Ellie. I have, like, three million throw pillows in all different colors, and they're *soooo* cozy.

"So tell me," I say.

"What's it worth?" Ellie asks.

"Ellie!"

"Okay, okay," she says. I can hear her stirring something in the background. Probably macaroni and cheese. Ellie's a vegetarian, and so she eats a lot of pasta. It's the only thing she really knows how to cook, and her mom refuses to make anything special for her. That's because Ellie has five brothers and sisters, and also because she has a reputation for abandoning her big ideas. But she's been a vegetarian for six whole months, which is pretty good. "So I was talking to Kyle."

"And?"

"And so I said, 'That was crazy, wasn't it, how Kendall's dad just showed up at the mall?'"

"Ellie!" I yell, burying my face into a pillow. "You didn't!"

Daniella, who's doing splits and stretches on my floor, rolls her eyes, like she can't believe whatever drama I have going on is even worth getting upset about. Which is annoying, but also kind of justified, since her drama of having to find out what's going on with Jen so she can move on to wherever it is she's supposed to go is def more serious than the crush I have on Brandon. Still. You'd think she'd be a little more supportive. Especially since I'm the only one who's going to be able to help her.

"I had to," Ellie says. "How else could I get it out in the open?"

"It didn't have to go out in the open!"

"Then how was I supposed to find out what Brandon thought about it?"

"I don't know," I say, chewing on my lip. "But there had to be a better way."

"Well, it doesn't matter," she says. "Because Brandon obviously didn't care. He was freaked out at first, but it's okay now."

"How do you know?"

"Because he told Kyle something."

"What did he tell Kyle?"

"He told him that he was going to ask you to hang out tomorrow!"

She shrieks, and I shriek, and Daniella almost falls off the bottom rail of my bed, which she's walking on like a balance beam. I guess Jen was right—Daniella definitely needs some more work when it comes to the balance beam.

Or maybe she just needs to work on her concentration. I mean, if a little shriek is going to get her so distracted that she falls off, she probably needs better focus.

"What should I wear?" I'm at my closet, flipping through everything, and there's nothing. Not one thing that is even close to being Brandon-asking-me-to-hang-out appropriate. I check the clock, wondering if it's too late to make an emergency trip to the mall.

"Your jean skirt?" Ellie asks.

"No."

"Ooh, how about that really pretty pearl-pink top with the layers of fabric?"

"Too fancy."

"How about your gray hoodie with the gold butterfly?"

"Not special enough."

"This is a total emergency," Ellie says. "We need to take inventory of your closet immediately."

We spend the rest of the night on the phone, putting together the perfect outfit for tomorrow, when Brandon maybe asks me out on my very first date ever. We decide on an emerald-green top with a boatneck, a white skirt, and Ellie's gold ballet flats. I'll do my hair in a messy bun and slide gold sparkly chopsticks through the top.

By the time we're done picking out makeup colors (soft pink lip gloss and a creamy silver eye shadow that isn't too dramatic, since my dad will totally flip if he sees me leaving

63

the house in too much makeup), I finish up my homework and then climb into bed.

And as I'm drifting off to sleep, all I can think about is Brandon Dunham.

Scrape. Scratch. Scrape. Scratch.

Something that sounds like a piece of furniture being moved across the room wakes me up. I look at my alarm clock. Two thirty a.m. Ugh.

"Daniella," I moan, "you better not be practicing any kind of gymnastics moves on my furniture. You're going to wake my dad up." For some reason ghosts start to solidify more after midnight. That's why people are always claiming that ghosts come out at night. It's not that the ghosts only come out then, it's just that they become more visible. And it explains how some ghosts can move things when it gets late. They're stronger and have more physical presence at night.

Scrape. Scratch. Scrape.

"Daniella!" I say, and pull my pillow over my head. "I'm serious! If you get caught by a human, I won't be able to help you. You'll have to live in limbo forever." This is a lie, but I'm hoping she won't know that and will go to sleep. Not that ghosts need sleep. But couldn't she just read a book or something? I guess not, since her fingers would probably just slip through the pages. Maybe she should go spy on her old boyfriend whatshisname, the one she saw at the mall with another girl. That would serve him right, getting haunted, ha-ha-ha-ha.

Scrape. Scratch. It's louder now, and coming from my bookshelf.

I turn over and throw one of my pillows in that direction, even though I know it's not going to do anything. "Daniella!" I say, trying to keep my voice quiet so that I don't wake my dad. "Stop it!"

But to my surprise the shadowy figure in the corner is not Daniella. It's a woman, about forty years old or so, and she's looking through my bookshelf, scraping my books back and forth as she goes. Wow. She must be a really strong ghost. Two thirty in the morning or not, the fact that she can move books is impressive. In fact, I don't think I've ever seen a ghost that could do that.

I swallow. Usually I'm not scared when I see ghosts, because they've just always been there. But something about this one is a little . . . intense. The way she's moving those books is kind of creepy. Like I said, I've never seen a ghost do that before. She must have some serious unfinished business, to have all that energy. And she's not even looking at the books. She's looking at me.

"Go away," I say, and put my head under my pillow again. I try to keep my voice even so she won't be able to tell how freaked out I am. "I'm already busy, so, um, you should find someone else to help you." It's not even a lie. The last thing I need is another ghost bothering me. I have my hands full with crazy Daniella. Not to mention that I'm supposed to be getting my beauty sleep so that I can be ready to get asked out on my very first date ever tomorrow. I close my eyes tight and try to calm my heart, which is suddenly beating really fast.

But the ghost doesn't go away. She floats over to my bed. She's actually very fashionable, wearing skinny jeans and a tunic in a dark gray swirly pattern. Her hair is swept back off her face, and she's wearing tons of long necklaces.

"You," she says, and points her index finger at me. "*You* need to be on the green paper." She sounds very . . . sinister, and my heart catches in my throat.

"Hi," I say. "Um, I'm really sorry, but I'm already in the middle of solving one mystery. So I'm afraid I'm going to have to ask you to ask someone else for help." I have my covers pulled all the way up to my chin, and I cross my fingers under the blanket, hoping she'll go away.

"ADD YOURSELF TO THE GREEN PAPER," she says, her voice getting all screechy.

"I'm sorry," I say firmly. "But I don't know what that means."

"You," she says again. "Kendall. You must be on the green paper." My heart is beating so fast, it feels like it's going to come out of my chest, and my mouth goes dry.

How does she know my name? I wonder if I should scream for my dad. But what would I tell him? That a ghost is freaking me out? But maybe if he came into my room she'd go away.

I sit up and get ready to scream, but before I can, the ghost disappears. I collapse back against the pillows. But I'm so keyed up that I can't go back to sleep. I lie awake for a long time, and the only way I'm finally able to fall asleep is by keeping the light on all night.

Chapter

6

When I wake up the next morning, I decide to do my best to put what happened last night right out of my head. I have enough going on, thank you very much, without worrying about some creepy ghost.

Still, it's easier said than done. I keep thinking about the ghost while I get dressed for school, about how she was so insistent that I add myself to the green paper. I've never had anything like that happen to me before.

Whatever, I think as I do my hair for school. Ghosts are always saying things that don't make sense. Most of the time they're completely out of their minds. I mean, look at Daniella. She can't remember anything about her life, and she's always talking about things that are slightly nonsensical.

Besides, I look way too cute to be worried about ghosts. The outfit Ellie and I picked out last night looks fab, and my hair is cooperating perfectly. By the time I'm done getting ready, I'm starting to feel a little more calm, and I bound downstairs. I say good morning to my dad, then pour myself a huge bowl of cereal. I'm going to need my energy if I'm going to get through the excitement of the day.

"You look nice," my dad says.

"Thanks."

"This wouldn't have anything to do with that boy I saw you at the mall with, would it?"

"No," I lie. Talk about awkward. How am I supposed to tell my dad that I like Brandon? Or that I like any boys at all? Ohmigod. I just realized something. How am I going to tell my dad that I'm going out on a date if Brandon *does* ask me? I mean, my dad has never really said I *couldn't* date, but maybe that's because he assumes that I already know I can't. But since he never said I couldn't . . . Wow, this is confusing. And humiliating. Oh, well. I'm not going to miss hanging out with Brandon just because of a potentially awkward conversation with my dad. I take a deep breath and decide to just go for it.

"So, Dad," I say, trying to sound all nonchalant. "If my outfit did, you know, *hypothetically*, have something to do with the boy you saw me with the other day, how would you feel about that?" This is something I've learned works with my dad. If I ask him how he feels about something, it's different than asking him for permission. It opens up a dialogue instead of setting him up as the authority figure. It's actually a very mature thing to do.

"Well," my dad says. He's cracking eggs into a bowl so that he can make his morning omelette. My dad has a western omelette every morning. He's supposed to only have egg whites, but sometimes he lets a little bit of yolk slip in. "I suppose I would want to know exactly what's going on with you and this boy."

Don't we all, I think. "Weeelll, what if he was maybe going to ask me to hang out?" I ask. "Could I hang out with him?" "Hang out" sounds way less intimidating than "date." Even though, of course, that's what it would be. Wouldn't it? Is it possible Brandon's just going to ask me to hang out because he wants to be friends? That would be horrible, and so I push it out of my mind, right into some mental "ignore" folder, like where I decided to put that woman ghost from last night.

"Like a date?" my dad asks. He's frowning suspiciously into the frying pan.

"Or maybe, like, a group thing, or a study session or something."

My dad hesitates. And then, finally, he says, "I guess that would be okay."

Daniella appears beside me and rolls her eyes. "God,

70

your dad is, like, *sooo* overprotective. I was going out on dates all the time when I was thirteen." She thinks about it. "Of course, I was getting asked out constantly, so it made sense." Ugh.

"Thanks, Dad," I say, deciding to ignore Daniella's comment. *Today is going to be great,* I tell myself. Then I grab my bag and head out the door to catch the bus, Daniella trailing along behind me.

Okay. I really need to calm down. I mean, there's no reason to get all riled up just because Brandon might ask me to hang out. I don't even know if it's going to happen for sure. Kyle is definitely not the best source of information. He probably forgets things, or messes things up all the time. Especially important things like who his best friend is going to ask to hang out.

Still. I can't help getting butterflies in my stomach about it, and all morning I keep my eyes peeled for Brandon. When I pass him in the hall after third period, he says, "Hi," and I feel my insides melt. But he doesn't ask me to hang out. Maybe he's waiting until later, when we have more time to talk?

By the time math rolls around, I am officially freaking out. I stopped off at the bathroom to reapply my lip gloss and reposition the chopsticks in my hair. Even so, I'm so wound up and jumpy that I'm one of the first people in the classroom.

"Well, Ms. Williams," Mr. Jacobi says. "You're here early."

"Yup," I say, holding up my notebook. "Here and ready to learn!"

"Good," he says. And I'm not sure, but I think I hear him mumble under his breath, "You need all the help you can get." Which is pretty rude when you think about it. Just because some of us aren't so good at math, that doesn't give him the right to make comments about it. Not to mention that he's a teacher, and teachers really shouldn't be snarky about students. . . .

Ohmigod. It's Brandon. Brandon is walking in! He's wearing khaki pants and this navy-blue long-sleeved T-shirt, and his hair is a little bit messy, but in a really cute, rumpled kind of way, and my heart does a flip and my stomach gets even more butterflies.

"Hmmm," Daniella says, wrinkling up her nose and putting her hands on her hips as she watches Brandon walk into the room. "I guess he's okay. I mean, if you like that type."

"Shut up," I whisper at her. The last thing I need is some ghost messing up my maybe-getting-asked-on-my-first-date-ever conversation.

"What?" Brandon asks. He's over by my desk now. "Did you just tell me to shut up?"

"Um, no." I laugh and reach my hand up to twirl my

hair before I realize it's in a bun. Oops. "Why would I have told you to shut up?"

"I don't know," he says, "since I didn't say anything. But I'm pretty sure I just heard you tell someone to shut up." He looks around the classroom. Besides us and Mr. Jacobi, there are only two other people in the room, and they're all the way on the other side, near the windows.

"You must have been hearing things," I say. Then I bat my eyelashes and smile at him in an effort to keep him distracted.

"I guess." But he looks doubtful.

Daniella laughs. "Great," she says. "Now he thinks you're crazy. You better change the subject, pronto."

I want to give her a dirty look, but I figure Brandon seeing me glare into the air definitely isn't a good way to change his mind about the fact that I might be crazy, so instead I say, "So did you do the homework?"

"Yeah," he says. "You?"

"Yup." I did it last night, after picking out my clothes. Although I had a really hard time concentrating. "I don't know how well I did, though."

"I'm sure you did great."

"No," I say, sighing. "I don't think I did."

And then Brandon blushes. Seriously, his face gets all red. "Well," he says, "I could probably help you with it."

"I think it's too late for that," I say. "The homework's already done."

Daniella smacks her hand against her forehead, like she can't believe how stupid I'm being. Which is ridiculous, since I'm not being stupid. Does she really expect that I can just do my homework all over before the bell rings in a minute? Just because she's older and probably thinks the quadratic formula is super-easy doesn't mean she has the right to just—

"No, I mean . . ." Brandon clears his throat. "I mean, I could help you study. You could maybe come over after school today."

Oh. My. God. This is it! Brandon Dunham is asking me to hang out, just like Ellie said he was going to!

"Sure," I say, all casual, even though a million fireworks are going off in my stomach. "That could be cool."

"Cool," he says, letting out a breath in one big whoosh. Is it possible he was nervous about asking me to hang out? "So, um, can you ride my bus home with me?"

"Yeah," I say. "I'll just have to ask my dad." He'll say yes, right? He has to!

He does. Say yes, I mean. The only problem? He has, like, five million different conditions, including the following:

He has to pick me up before dinner. Which is actually fine with me, since I don't really want to have to eat dinner with Brandon and his family. I mean, that would be kind of awkward, wouldn't it? I'd be so nervous! What if his mom didn't like me? What if I left and she was all, "Brandon! I cannot believe you brought that girl home. I think my son can do a lot better than *her.* She had some sort of ridiculous chopsticks in her hair!" And then Brandon would be like, "Mom, you're right. I think I'm going to ask someone else out, someone with more normal hair who's smarter at math."

My dad has to be able to call Brandon's parents to make sure it's okay with them and that they're going to be home. Which is actually a little bit insulting, because there's no way that I would lie to my dad about Brandon's parents being home. But I guess since I lied to him the other day about being at the library, he's kind of suspicious of me. And I guess I deserve it. The good thing is that Brandon doesn't even care that my dad wants to talk to his parents, and he texts me his dad's cell number so that my dad can call him. Yay!

My dad called Cindy to ask if she thought it was okay for me to go to Brandon's. (This one isn't actually a condition, but it should def still be on the list since it *is* a problem.) Luckily, it sounded like Cindy was all for it and told my dad it was perfectly normal for me to be interested in hanging out with boys and blah, blah, blah. I'm glad she said yes, but I really do *not* want my dad to check in with Cindy every time I want to do something. And her getting involved in my love life, even if she is on my side, is a little too close for comfort.

"Whatever you do, don't kiss him first," Daniella says to me on the way out of school. I almost choke on my Jolly Rancher.

"Who said anything about kissing?" I say. "There's not going to be any kissing. We're just going to be studying!"

She gives me a look like *That's what you think*, which starts the fireworks in my stomach all over again.

"When are you going to be able to go back and talk to Jen again?" she asks as we walk through the crowd of kids in the hallway. Luckily, it's so loud and crazy that no one notices that I seem to be talking to myself.

"I don't know. Tomorrow, maybe? Oh, no, wait. I can't tomorrow. Ellie has a dance recital, and I promised her I'd go." I shift my bag onto my other arm. "And let's get back to the kissing, please."

"A dance recital?" Daniella says, obviously so self-centered that she can't focus on the more important issue, i.e., the potential kissing that could take place at Brandon's. "Kendall, my moving on to wherever it is I'm supposed to go is more important than some stupid dance recital."

"It's not stupid," I say. "And besides, I need to give Jen a cooling-off period. She thinks I'm psychotic."

"She doesn't need to cool off!" Daniella says. She puts her hands on her hips. "You need to do something! You know, this isn't very fair, you just taking off to hang out with boys when you could be helping me. You're pretty self-ish, Kendall."

"No, I'm not," I say, keeping my voice steady, even though all I want to do is yell at her. "You don't understand how this works. You need to trust me."

But before she can say anything back, she just . . . fades away. I guess I stressed her out. Whatever. I don't even feel that bad about it, because she doesn't know what she's talking about. The last thing I need is for Jen to start thinking I'm some kind of stalker or something. What if she calls the police? Or tells her parents that I've been bothering her, and then they call my dad? I mean, talk about a big fat mess. And what's up with Daniella calling me selfish? I'm trying to help her, but it's going to take time. She needs to chill.

"Hey," Brandon says, walking up to where I'm standing at the side of the school in front of the row of buses. "You ready?"

"Yes," I say. I smooth down my shirt and start following him to his bus. It's weird, being out here with Brandon, in front of everyone. I mean, everyone around us is just passing by, on their way to their own buses, not really paying any attention to us. I was kind of hoping that they'd at least *notice* we were together. Not that it's important for people to notice us. It would just be, you know, more dramatic.

"Bus pass?" the bus driver asks when I step on. And she

doesn't sound too happy about it either. There's a moment when I panic, because I seem to have misplaced my pass, but after a few minutes and a few sighs, I find it underneath the cover of one of my notebooks.

There aren't enough empty seats on the bus, so Brandon and I can't sit together. I'm disappointed at first (how cute would it be for us to be sitting together, knees touching, heads together while we talk?), but then I realize it's actually okay, since it gives me time to collect my thoughts.

I end up sitting with this girl June Melfi, who is pretty annoying and kind of a blabbermouth, but her constant chatter calms me down, and by the time we get to Brandon's house, I'm not nervous at all. Well, maybe a little. But nowhere near what I was earlier.

I text Ellie right before I get off the bus. *At B's house! Will cll u later xxo.*

And then I take a deep breath and follow Brandon off the bus and into his house.

"Brandon has a *girrrrrllll* over." Hmmm. Brandon failed to mention he has a crazy little sister. Seriously, I think the girl might be a bit deranged. And that's saying a lot, coming from me. I mean, I can see ghosts.

First, it's how she's dressed. Like a ninja. Which is fine. I mean, I'm all for girl ninjas. But I do think that maybe you need to tone it down a little bit if you're having people over.

She's about one second away from karate-chopping me.

"Grace," Brandon says, taking off his coat and hanging it on the rack next to the door. "Please don't karate-chop Kendall."

"Yeah," I say. "I don't really want to be chopped." Brandon holds his hand out for my coat, and I hand it to him.

"What's the matter?" Grace taunts. "Are you afraid?" She gets into a karate stance and holds up her hands like she's ready for a good chop.

"No," I say, even though I kind of am. "I just don't feel like it right now."

"Dad!" Grace screams, suddenly turning around and galloping off into the living room. "Dad, Dad, Daddy! Brandon has his *girlllfriend* with him!"

God, this is way worse than the stuff I imagined about his mom not liking me. A crazy eight-year-old who thinks she's a ninja, and that I'm Brandon's girlfriend? Not that I mind being called his girlfriend. I sneak a look at him out of the corner of my eye, to see how he's reacting to being called my boyfriend. He seems a little . . . annoyed. Of course, that could definitely just be because Grace is annoying, and aren't all older brothers usually annoyed by their little sisters?

"Hello," Brandon's dad says, coming out of the living room to meet me and Brandon as we walk into the kitchen. He's tall, and he looks pretty much just like Brandon. He's wearing a flannel shirt spotted with paint, and he's blinking hard, like the light is bothering him. "Sorry, I was working and I got caught up." He looks down at his shirt with a confused look on his face, like he can't imagine where all that paint came from.

"Dad's an illustrator for children's books," Brandon explains, "and sometimes he gets lost in his work."

"That's okay," I say. "Hi, I'm Kendall. It's nice to meet you, Mr. Dunham."

"Please," he says, "call me John."

"Okay." Yay! John! He wants me to call him John! Already on a first-name basis with the dad! That can only be a good sign.

"Would you kids like a snack?" Mr. Dunham asks. He crosses the room to the refrigerator and peers inside. "We have a veggie tray with dip, some crackers . . ." He opens the freezer. "Frozen potato skins, frozen mozzarella sticks, frozen zucchini balls . . ."

Frozen zucchini balls? That doesn't sound all that appetizing. On the other hand, the rest of the frozen food sounds great. My dad never lets us have stuff like that. Well, usually not. That's mostly because Cindy sent him this article about how eating organic is so much better, and how if you let your children eat processed foods they go crazy and become serial killers. Of course, that doesn't stop him from sneaking stuff himself every once in a while.

"Potato skins?" Brandon asks, looking at me.

"Perfect." I grin. God, we are so in sync! It's like we have some kind of psychic connection. What are the chances that we'd both want potato skins?

"I'm going to have some too!" Grace screams. Then she pokes me with a plastic sword that she's pulled out from somewhere.

"No, Grace," Mr. Dunham (John?) says. "You and I are going to go into the living room and let Brandon and Kendall study in here."

"NO!" Grace says. "I. WANT. POTATO SKINS." She pokes me again with the sword, a little harder this time. Ouch.

"Grace," I try, "how about when the skins are ready, we bring you some? Would that be okay? And then maybe after Brandon and I are done with our homework, we can play ninja." Please, please, please let us have so much homework that we don't have time to play ninja.

"I'm not a ninja!" Grace says. "I'm a karate master."

"Well, then we can play karate master." I think about adding "just as long as I'm not the victim" but decide to get into the specifics later.

She thinks about it. "Okay," she finally says. Then she grabs her dad's hand. "Come on," she says. "I want to watch a movie."

Once they're gone, Brandon smiles at me apologetically.

"Sorry." He reaches down into one of the cabinets and pulls out a cookie sheet. I open the box of potato skins and start laying them neatly on the sheet as Brandon turns on the oven.

"Oh, it's no problem," I say. "She's cute." And she is. If you like hyperactivity. I don't, but whatevs. I can't exactly say that to him. No one wants to hear something bad about their little sister. Besides, why would I ruin this moment? It's so cozy in here, cooking with Brandon. I place another potato skin on the sheet and look around the kitchen.

It's done in butter yellow and white, and opens up into the dining room. It's cheerful and bright, and there's a picture of Brandon's family hanging on the wall in the dining room. How cute! It's a family portrait, with a light blue background and the whole family dressed up and smiling. Grace looks like she's about four, and Brandon's maybe nine? I wonder if my dad and I should get our picture taken to hang on the wall of our house. Like, a professional one. Of course, it would only be the two of us, so—

Oh. My. God. Ohmigod, ohmigod, ohmigod. I drop a potato skin onto the sheet and swallow hard. Because I just noticed something about the picture of Brandon and his family. It's his mom. Oh, she looks perfectly fine as far as moms go. Except for one thing. She's the ghost who was in my room last night, telling me to add myself to the green paper.

Chapter

7

Okay. There is no need to panic. First, it might not even be her. I actually have very bad eyesight sometimes. Especially when it's dark and I'm squinting and half asleep. It could have been anyone in my room. I mean, what are the chances that the ghost who showed up last night is BRANDON'S MOM? And that she would be so scary and aggressive?

That's just crazy. Especially since a ghost connected to someone I know has never come asking for help before. Not that I know that many people who've died. And not that I really know Brandon's mom. But still. A nagging thought comes into my head, one of those thoughts that you want to do your best to ignore but know you can't. A thought about how if Mrs. Dunham was able to move those books last night, her energy must be really intense. Which means that whatever she had to say might have something to do with my connection to Brandon. But that's ridiculous, right? Why would she be interested in me and Brandon?

And besides, like I said, it's probably not even her. And I definitely shouldn't bring it up to Brandon. Because what if it *is* her? It means his mom is dead, and he might not want to talk about it, and then it would get all weird and awkward and—

"I like that picture," I say, pointing at it. Jeez. Way to be smooth, Kendall. "That's, um, a nice picture of your family."

"Yeah," he says, and he looks a little sad. A little sad like maybe his mom died? No. I'm sure I'm imagining it. "My mom died a few years ago."

Well. That settles that. "Wow, I'm really sorry," I say.

He shrugs. "Yeah," he says. "She got sick, and then . . ." His voice trails off.

"That must have been . . . hard," I say. His voice is kind of catching, and so now mine is too. I want to tell him not to worry about it, that people who die are actually okay, that they're not in pain, that for the most part they're totally happy. But obviously I can't tell him that, because then he'll think I'm psycho.

"Yeah," he says. "She—"

"ARE THOSE POTATO SKINS DONE YET?" Grace

yells from the other room. "And you better not eat all the sour cream, Brandon and his girlfriend, I forget what your name is!"

"Don't worry," Brandon yells back. "We won't." He smiles. "Should we start studying while we wait for these to cook?"

"Sure," I say. I follow him to the table, my mind racing.

I cannot stop thinking about it. Brandon's mom showed up in my room! What did she want? What's her deal? Is she going to tell me something that has to do with Brandon? And why is she just showing up now, when usually the people I see are people who've died recently and need help with something so that they can move on? Has Brandon's mom been unable to move on for years? That's horrible! And what does she need help with?

I try to remember what she was talking about. Something having to do with the green paper. Green paper, green paper, green paper. Maybe money? What's something else that's green?

I should really have paid more attention. But honestly, I was way too scared. I just wanted her to go away. Even now, knowing that she's Brandon's mom, I kind of don't want her to come back.

I'm thinking about all of this during my study session with Brandon, which, by the way, goes very well. Brandon is a much better teacher than Mr. Jacobi, so by the end of the session, not only have I spent time with Brandon, but I actually think I'm finally getting a handle on some math stuff.

Still, it's hard not to be distracted, and as soon I get home from Brandon's house, I run upstairs and stand in the middle of my room.

"Ghost!" I yell. "Ghost of Mrs. Dunham, please come back here immediately!" I take a deep breath and get ready to face her.

But nothing happens. Crap. I decide to try again, "Ghost!" I yell. "Ghost of Mrs. Dunham, mother of Brandon Dunham, please show yourself!"

Still nothing. Except the sound of my dad rapping on the ceiling of the kitchen with a broom handle. Which is what he does when I'm being too loud. Well, there goes that plan. I can't have my dad hearing me scream like that. He'll send me to a psychiatrist, stat.

"What's all the yelling about?" Daniella asks.

"Oh," I say, "it's you." Figures that the ghost I *don't* want to see shows up, while the one I *do* want to see is nowhere to be found. I fling myself down onto my bed.

"Nice to see you, too," she says, rolling her eyes as she lounges in my desk chair. "How was your date?"

"Fine."

"Fine? All you're going to say about it is 'fine'? You were freaking out about it."

"I was not freaking out about it!" I say. Even though I kind of was.

"Did you kiss him?"

"None of your business!" My face flames. Because the truth is, we didn't kiss. It just wasn't that kind of vibe, really. I mean, his dad and his little sister were pretty much there the whole time. And even though we were studying, Grace kept running in and out of the kitchen.

Although there *was* a moment when Brandon was showing me how to do a problem, and then he leaned over to erase something on my paper, and when he did, our hands touched, and I think he left his hand on mine for, like, a couple seconds more than was really necessary. Ohmigod. If his dad wasn't there, would he have held my hand? Would he have kissed me? I've never kissed a boy before. Is it hard? Will I know what to do?

God, I really need some more lip gloss. And to talk to Ellie. She's kissed two boys before. Jason Michaels last year, and this boy at camp whose name I forget.

"It *is* my business," Daniella says. "Since you're spending all your time gallivanting around, flirting and kissing and doing God knows what, when you should be helping me!"

"For your information," I say, mostly because I want to get off the subject of me and Brandon kissing, "I was just about to tell you that I'm planning to go and try to talk to

Jen tomorrow." It's a lie, of course. I haven't been planning it. In fact, I just said it to shut her up.

"What about Ellie's dance recital?" she asks suspiciously.

"It's right after school," I say, "And so I'll have time to see Jen after."

"Okay!" she says, brightening. "What will you say to her?"

"I have no idea," I say. That part, at least, is the truth.

That night I get woken up again by Mrs. Dunham. When I open my eyes at three thirty in the morning, she's standing right over me. I shriek, but then force myself to bite it back, since I don't want my dad coming into my room. Even though I'm scared, I need to talk to her. Maybe it won't be that bad.

I prop myself up on my elbows and force myself to look at her. I'm surprised to find that Mrs. Dunham actually has a very kind face. She looks exactly like what you'd want the mom of your crush to look like. It's too bad she's not still alive. Maybe it's just death that's making her angry.

But then Mrs. Dunham says, "Put yourself on that green paper!" and she sounds really threatening, and I forget all about the fact that she has a kind-looking face.

At first I'm scared. But then I get angry. "You know," I say, sitting all the way up in bed, "it's pretty nervy of you to just show up here, being all threatening and not even telling me you're Brandon's mom! If you want me to do something about the green paper, you're going to have to tell me what it means."

But I think maybe I made Mrs. Dunham mad. Because her eyes narrow, and then, just when she looks like she's about to say something else, she fades away.

The next morning Ellie is standing at my locker, waiting for me and jumping up and down, looking excited. "I have to tell you something, I have to tell you something, I have to tell you something!" she says.

"English office?" I ask. I'm a little grumpy, since I had a hard time falling back asleep last night after Mrs. Dunham left. At least it's Friday. Hopefully I'll be able to catch up on my sleep this weekend.

"Yes."

We head to the English office, and when we get there, Mrs. D'Amico is sitting at her desk, grading papers. "Hi, girls," she says, smiling at us. "Your hair looks fabulous, Kendall."

"Thank you," I say. Today I decided to go a little less crazy, and so I wore my hair in two French braids down the back, with a string of tinsel through each one. Kind of classic, but still with a little flair. It completely fits my mood—mostly calm but with a little frisson of electricity sliding through me.

"Do you girls want a coffee?" Mrs. D'Amico asks.

Ellie wrinkles up her nose, but I head over to the coffee machine and start brewing a cup.

"How's everything going?" Mrs. D'Amico asks.

"Fine," we chorus.

"I saw you leaving yesterday with Brandon Dunham, Kendall," she says, stirring her coffee with one of those plastic stir sticks. "He's quite the fox."

I blush. "Mrs. D'Amico!"

"What?" she asks. "I can't say that you have good taste in men?" I don't have the heart to point out that Brandon's not really a man, and also that no one uses the word "fox" anymore. "Well," she says, smiling, "I think your grandmother would approve."

"I think so too," I say, thinking of how much Gram would have liked Brandon.

"Anyway," Mrs. D'Amico says, standing up and gathering up her coffee and her grade book. "I'll leave you girls alone. Just make sure you're not late to homeroom."

"Okay," Ellie says once it's just the two of us. "So I have good news and I have bad news. Which do you want first?"

"Um, bad news, I guess." It's always better to start with bad news. That way, when you get the good news, it hopefully can erase the bad feelings you're having after hearing the bad news.

"The bad news is that Kyle asked Brandon how it was

90

hanging out with you yesterday." Ellie chews on her bottom lip. My heart squeezes into a tight lump.

"And what did he say?" I whisper, bracing myself.

"He said that it was okay."

"*Okay?* He said that it was *okay*?" I grab my cup of coffee off the machine and dump seven sugars into it. Okay?! It was way more than okay. I guess he forgot to mention the fact that he almost held my hand at one point.

"Yeah." Ellie's still chewing on her lip. I decide this calls for peppermint mocha creamer, and I dump so much into my coffee that it's basically half coffee, half cream. Oh, well. I love peppermint lattes.

"Well, what do you think that means?" I ask.

"Well," Ellie says slowly, "I think it means that he probably thought it was just okay."

"What a disaster," I say, flinging myself down onto my cozy red chair.

"I thought you said it was fun," Ellie says. Yesterday after dinner I spent, like, two hours on the phone with Ellie, dissecting the whole afternoon and going over it second by second, including the part where Brandon almost held my hand.

"It was!" I say, swinging my legs over the arm of the chair and taking a big sip of my coffee. "But I guess he didn't think so. Quick, tell me the good news before I die." I'm nothing if not dramatic. And the good news better be good. Good enough to pull me out of my funk.

"The good news," Ellie says, flushing, "is that Kyle asked me to go to the movies with him tonight."

"*That's* the good news?" I say before I can stop myself. Then I realize how that must sound. Like I'm a bad friend. I really am glad that she's going to the movies with Kyle, but at the same time, how is that supposed to make me feel better?

"Yeah," she says, and looks down at the floor. "I'm sorry, Kendall. I probably should have picked another time to tell you. I was just really excited."

"No, *I'm* sorry," I say. "I shouldn't have reacted like that. I just got thrown off guard when you told me that about Brandon." I wonder how it will be in math. Will he completely ignore me? Will I completely ignore him? Will other people in the class be able to tell there's something weird going on between us? I wonder if Mr. Jacobi will let me switch my seat.

"Yeah, I know," Ellie says. "But try not to be too bummed. I mean, who knows if Kyle even knows what he's talking about? Boys don't listen to what people are telling them half the time anyway."

"Yeah," I say. I sip at my coffee, then smile through my disappointment, determined to be happy for Ellie. "So, what movie are you guys going to see?"

"Not sure," she says, her face flushed. "But I hope something romantic."

We spend the rest of the time before homeroom talking

about what she's going to wear (jeans, glittery ballet flats, ruffly white T-shirt, pink sparkly sweater). Although, if I'm being completely honest, my mind is only half on the conversation. The rest of it is obsessing over Brandon, and trying to ignore Daniella, who has popped up and is moaning about how much she misses coffee. Ugh.

But when I get to math later that day, I'm feeling a lot better, since I've had some time to get over it.

I know I look fabulous—the two French braids, plus skinny jeans, plus a deep crimson V-neck sweater that looks like cashmere even though it isn't, and a super-cute mint-green and maroon scarf. This morning I decided to dress up so that Brandon would remember how amazing I am and how fun our date was yesterday. But now I've decided it's so I can show him what he's missing.

I'm way too strong to get upset over some boy. I mean, I'm only in seventh grade! There are going to be way more boys in my future. Boys that I'm going to meet this year, boys that I'm going to have crushes on in eighth grade, boys that I'm going to date in high school and college, and a boy I'm going to marry someday. And that boy is *not* going to be Brandon Dunham. Besides, his mom is so scary, it would definitely put a crimp in our relationship.

In fact, I've decided to ignore him completely. If he thinks he can just tell someone that hanging out with me was "okay," then, well, he has another thing coming. And if he thinks that he's the only one who can help me with my math, then he *really* has another thing coming.

I plop down in my seat, happy to have that settled. And as soon as Brandon starts walking into the room, I turn my back to him and say really loudly to Arianna Wintchel, "Hey, Arianna, what'd you get on the last test?"

"Um, a hundred." She looks a little confused, probably because she and I don't talk that much. Plus I'm asking her about her grade, which is pretty random. Not that it's that big of a secret. She's one of the smartest kids in our grade.

"Fab," I say. "So do you think you can tutor me?"

"Oh, God," Daniella says. She rolls her eyes. "Trying to make guys jealous never works, just fyi." I glare at her. What does she know about boys, anyway? Last time I saw her interact with a boy, she was screaming at someone in a food court even though she's dead and he couldn't hear her.

Brandon's at his desk now, and he says, "Wait a minute! What's wrong with me? I'm not a good tutor?"

"You're *okay*." I put the emphasis on "okay" so that he knows I'm onto him. I will not stand for a pity conversation. And I don't want him to think that I had a great time, even though I did. I mean, I do have *some* pride. I flip one of my braids over my shoulder haughtily.

"Well, I'll have to improve," he says, smiling.

"Hmmph," I say, determined not to be swayed by his dimples and amazing smile.

"So listen," he says, "Kyle and Ellie are going to a movie tonight. Do you think your dad might let you go with me?"

Whaaa-aaa? "Wait, what?" I shake my head, wondering if I've misheard him.

"God, you're hopeless," Daniella says, rolling her eyes.

"A movie," Brandon says, a little slower this time. "I'm not sure which one yet, but it'll be fun to hang out no matter what we see."

"Um, sure," I say, even though I'm totally thrown and confused. Why is he asking me to a movie when he told Kyle it was just okay hanging out with me? Is it possible Kyle really did get the story wrong? Or maybe it's just a boy thing? This is all *sooo* confusing!

"Oh! And Grace told me to give you this." Brandon reaches into his bag and pulls out a piece of paper. On it is a crayon drawing of two girl ninjas. One has a big arrow pointing to it that says "Grace" and the other one says "Kendall."

How sweet! I put the drawing in my bag. Things are totally looking up.

Chapter

8

"So, what do you think it means?" I ask into the phone, peering through the bushes. It's after school, after Ellie's dance recital (which she was totally fab in, btw), and I'm back at the high school, gearing up for another run-in with Jen. After what happened last time, I know she's going to be less than thrilled to see me, so I had to plan a sneak attack.

"I don't know!" Ellie says through the receiver. "Want me to ask Kyle about it?"

"No!" I say. "I think I'll just maybe wait until tonight and see how things go." The last thing I need is Kyle getting the story messed up again and causing me all kinds of undue mental stress. Not to mention that I need to be mature about this. If I have a question about how Brandon feels about me, then I should ask him myself, right? Of course, that's easier said than done.

"Oooh, that's a good idea," Ellie says. "Take it slow and cool."

"Now, when you see her," Daniella's saying, "try to be nice. Jen's very laid-back, but when she gets mad, she really gets mad. So just, you know, take it easy." She's jumping up and down next to me, doing some kind of stretch. I don't know *why* she thinks it's okay to talk to me when I'm obviously in the middle of a very important phone conversation—I mean, rude much?—so I ignore her.

"Are you still going to wear what we planned?" I ask Ellie.

"Yeah."

"Good, because I don't want to show up in something too similar to yours. How humiliating would it be if they thought we planned to dress like twins?"

"Soo humiliating," she says.

"Dressing like twins is ridiculous," Daniella reports, then kicks her legs up into a handstand. I decide not to mention the fact that Ellie and I do dress alike sometimes, just for fun, like if we go shopping together and fall in love with the same outfit. I don't get what the big deal is if it's just a random Tuesday at school. Obviously I would never do it on a date or anything, because that's definitely a little bit ridiculous, but—

"There she is!" Daniella yells, pointing. Jen's walking across the other side of the parking lot.

"Crap," I say. I thought she'd be coming out the door over here, near where the late buses are. But maybe she's getting a ride, or she's going somewhere else. "Ellie," I say, "I have to go."

"Why?" she asks.

"I just do. So, listen, I'll meet you at the theater at six forty-five?"

"Okay," she says. "We can hang out in the bathroom for twenty minutes and reapply our lip gloss. That way we'll be five minutes late."

"Perfect," I say, "and you really were amazing at your recital."

I hang up my phone and go charging across the parking lot like some kind of crazy woman.

"So much for being calm," Daniella says, keeping up with me like it's nothing. Of course, she is a ghost. So it's not like she gets winded or anything.

"Oh, hello," I say when I catch up with Jen. I slow down a little so that I'm walking right behind her.

She turns around and looks at me, a smile on her face. Then, when she sees who it is (aka me), she immediately turns back around and starts walking faster.

"Wait!" I say, doubling my stride to keep up with her. She's really fast for someone so short. "I just want to apologize. Please!" She keeps walking. Then I realize I'm going to have to bring in some of my acting skills if I want this to work. I decide to pretend I'm a clueless middle school girl. Which I guess I kind of am. "Jen," I say, "please accept my apology. I would just die if I thought you were mad at me." At the end I put a little sniffle into my voice, like maybe I'm about to start crying.

She turns around, slowing down just a little. "I'm not mad at you," she says. But it doesn't really sound like it's the truth.

"Oh, thank goodness," I say, giving her my best smile. "Because I would really just die if I thought the best gymnast I knew was mad at me."

"I thought Daniella was the best gymnast you knew," she says.

I smile. But this time I've done my homework. "Daniella was *technically* perfect," I say. "At the vault. And the floor exercise. Even when she struggled on the beam, you could see her athleticism. But there's so much more that goes into being a good gymnast. Heart. And pushing through injuries." Jen looks at me, and her face softens.

"Oh, God," Daniella says, rolling her eyes. "That's laying it on a little thick, don't you think? And I *do* push through injuries! Didn't you hear the story she told about the time I pretty much got a concussion?"

But Jen's eating it up. "Yeah," she says, "that's true." She shifts her gym bag on her shoulder, then reaches down and zips up the hoodie she's wearing. "Look, I'm sorry if I was hard on you the other day. It's just that ever since Daniella died, it's been really hard for me, you know? I don't know who to trust."

"I understand," I say.

"Oh, please," Daniella says. "She doesn't know who to trust? It's not like I left her a million dollars or something."

"You'd be surprised how many people try to talk to me just because they want to know the details of what happened that night," Jen says. "It's creepy, you know?"

I wonder what she'd think if I told her I could see dead people, and that her dead friend is in this parking lot with us and has been talking nonsense about something having to do with her and a shovel. Probably she wouldn't be too thrilled.

"That makes sense," I say. "I know that a lot of times when I tell people my mom left, they act all concerned, but really they just want to know the gossip."

"Your mom left?"

"Yeah," I say. I decide to leave it at that. She doesn't need to know that my mom left when I was so little that I don't even remember her. And that even if people did want to know gossip about it, I don't know any.

"I'm really sorry."

"'S okay," I mumble, and then look down at my shoes. God, I am getting a lot better at this acting thing. It used to not work so well, if you want to know the truth. In fact, one time my subpar acting skills got me kicked out of a mini-mart by the police. (I won't get into it, but the ghost I was helping had a dad who ran the store.) I add in another sniffle for good measure.

"Hey, don't cry," Jen says, sighing. She rummages through her bag for a tissue, and then hands it to me. I pretend to blow my nose.

Daniella's mouth drops open. "Wow. You are actually really good at this."

"Thanks," I say to Jen. And Daniella. Even though I do feel kind of bad. I mean, I shouldn't really be playing on the poor girl's emotions. Especially since her friend died not that long ago. But I tell myself that I'm helping Daniella, and that's more important. And in the process maybe I'll be helping Jen, too.

"Well," Jen says, "um, good luck with your gymnastics."

"Yeah," I say. "Good luck to you, too."

And then Jen walks away and gets into her car.

"That's it?" Daniella screams. "You didn't find out anything!"

Obviously she doesn't know the most important part of acting—knowing when to end the scene.

. . .

"My hair is a mess," I moan, looking at it in the mirror over the sinks.

"*Your* hair?" Ellie cries. "What about mine?"

"Your hair looks perfect, as usual," I say honestly. We've been in the bathroom of the movie theater for fifteen minutes now, which means we only have five more minutes until we have to meet the boys if we're going to stick to our be-five-minutes-late plan. And I'm nowhere near ready.

It's a miracle I even got here on time. My idea was to kind of blindside my dad with the whole going-to-the-movies-on-a-date thing at dinner so that he wouldn't really have time to think up a million reasons why I couldn't go. Also, I figured that by telling him the truth, it would show that I was capable and responsible. And the fact that Ellie and Kyle were going was, like, a bonus.

Of course, he had to call Cindy to find out what she thought, which was über-annoying, but whatevs. Cindy said it was okay, so I couldn't be too mad at her. Although I'm still a little mad at my dad for giving her so much power in our lives. It's like just because Cindy is a woman, he thinks she knows everything related to raising a daughter. But it doesn't mean she knows anything—especially about dating. My dad needs to learn to trust himself a little more. I'm turning out perfectly fine. I don't need a woman role model. Although, if my dad was relying on himself to make the decisions, he really might have said no. So I guess I shouldn't complain too much.

I survey myself in the mirror. Skinny jeans. Boots with a low heel. White sweater that's off the shoulder. Very cute, but also casual. "Okay," I say after smoothing my hair one more time. "I'm ready. You?"

"Yes." Ellie and I look at each other and squeal.

We walk out to meet the boys, and Brandon looks sooo cute in his jeans and black sweater. We stand in front of the concession stand, having a huge discussion about what to eat. Kyle wants to get Junior Mints, Swedish Fish, nachos, ice cream, and a hot dog. Which he does. And it comes to, like, fifty dollars, which is crazy. (Also, where did Kyle get all that money? My dad gave me a twenty and told me to bring back the change.)

But the real problem comes when Brandon and I order our snacks. A medium popcorn and a soda for me, a red slushie and a package of Reese's Pieces for Brandon. Which isn't the problem. The problem is that since it's Friday night, the theater is so packed that there's this huge long line, and so when it's our turn to order, the girl working the stand rings us up together. And then there's this totally awkward moment when Brandon hands her twenty dollars and I don't know if it's supposed to be for my stuff *and* his stuff or just his stuff.

So then I reach into my purse and hand over twelve

dollars, but then Brandon says, "Don't worry. I got it." Which makes me blush, and makes the girl behind the counter smirk, like I have no idea what I'm doing. So then I start to think that maybe *Brandon* thinks I have no idea what I'm doing, or worse, that maybe he thinks that *I* don't think this is a date. And then I remember how Ellie said that he said doing homework together was just okay, and I realize I still haven't gotten to the bottom of that, which makes me nervous.

So by the time we get into the theater, I'm kind of on edge. The only good thing is that Daniella isn't here. I'm not sure exactly where she went. Maybe she figured the night would be boring. Not that I'm complaining. The last thing I need is her here, making her little comments and getting me more anxious than I already am.

"Where should we sit?" Brandon asks.

"I usually sit halfway up and to the side," I say.

"I like sitting in front," Kyle says. He takes a bite of his nachos. "That way you're closer to the action."

"We always sit in the middle and to the side," Ellie says firmly.

"Whatever." Kyle shrugs.

When we sit down, somehow it works out that I'm sitting closest to the wall, followed by Brandon, followed by Kyle, followed by Ellie. This seating arrangement is horrible for a few reasons. One, because Ellie and I aren't sitting next to each other, so we can't whisper to each other about anything scandalous that might happen. And two, because now I'm stuck near the wall. Which means that if I have to go to the bathroom, I have to climb over all three of them. And I know it's not a big deal, that everyone goes to the bathroom, but something about it just seems super-embarrassing, you know?

I don't think I'm going to make it through the rest of the night, but once the lights go down and the first preview starts, Brandon leans in close and says, "I love the previews."

"Really?" I say. "I've never really been a fan."

"Really?" He seems shocked. "Why not?"

"Too much like commercials," I whisper, and take a handful of popcorn.

"Yeah, but you get to see what movies are coming out," he says. "So you know what to see."

"True," I say. "But if I want to know what to see, I'll just watch the preview online or something. The previews have always been kind of boring to me."

"That's because you've never watched them with me," he says. "I have a whole system." He explains that for every preview you have to give the preview itself—not the movie—either a thumbs-up or a thumbs-down. Fun!

For the most part we agree about the previews. We give two of them a thumbs-down, one a thumbs-up, and then

105

are split on the last two, a romantic comedy that I think looks really good but Brandon claims looks really silly, and an action movie that has way too many explosions for my taste, but which Brandon seems really excited about.

I like that we don't agree on every preview, because I think it would be boring to be with someone that agreed with you about everything.

"You want some popcorn?" I ask Brandon as the lights dim even further and the opening credits of the movie start. He reaches into the carton and my heart speeds up. I am sharing popcorn with Brandon Dunham! I've never shared popcorn with a boy before. It feels very scandalicious.

About five minutes into the movie, Brandon takes my hand. His hand is nice, warm and soft and not at all sweaty. Pulses of electricity fly up my fingers and rush through my body, and I lean my head against his shoulder. When the movie's finally over, I pretty much have no idea what it was about. I couldn't keep my mind on it. I just keep thinking about Brandon's closeness, and the fact that we were holding hands.

When the lights go up, I look over to see Ellie and Kyle sitting ramrod straight in their seats. Ellie has this super-blank look on her face, and Kyle's scowling at the floor. Uh-oh. I try to catch Ellie's eye, but she's staring straight ahead, not looking at me.

We all traipse up the aisle and into the lobby.

"I'm going to go call my mom," Ellie says. "To tell her we're ready to be picked up."

"Want me to go with you?" I ask.

"No," she says, "I'll be right back." She heads over to the spot between the front doors so that she can get away from the noise in the lobby.

"I'm going to play a video game," Kyle mumbles, walking over to where the arcade games are.

"What's up with those two?" Brandon asks.

"I don't know," I say.

"Well, Kyle can be kind of difficult."

"Yeah," I say. And then I can't take it anymore. I have to know, I have to ask him. "Hey," I say, "can I ask you something?"

"Sure."

"Well . . . I don't want to get Kyle in trouble or anything, but Kyle told Ellie that you said we just had an okay time when I was at your house yesterday." He gets an uncomfortable look on his face, so I rush on, "And that's fine. Really, I'm not mad. It's just . . . Well, I had a really nice time, so I was kind of confused."

"I had a great time too," Brandon says. "I really did. It's just that I wasn't sure you did because you seemed to get a little weird when I brought up the stuff about my mom."

Ohmigod. He noticed! He knew! And here I am, thinking I'm such a good actress, and it turns out it's not even true. Jeez. "Oh," I say dumbly, because I don't know what else to say.

"It's okay," he says, and then squeezes my hand. "A lot of people get a little weird about it, but I don't want you to have to feel uncomfortable, you know? It's really sad, but we don't have to avoid the topic or anything."

"Yeah," I say, "I guess I did get a little uncomfortable." What a lie! If anyone is comfortable with the idea of people dying, it's me. I mean, I have to be. Of course, it's really sad that Brandon doesn't have his mom around anymore. And I do feel really bad about that, and I think it's amazing how well he's doing. I didn't know my mom, but I can't imagine what it would have been like if I'd had her around for nine years of my life and then she died. That's one of the only positives about her leaving when I was so little. A lot of times I feel like if she'd stuck around longer, it would have been harder because I would have missed her more.

"You don't have to be uncomfortable," Brandon says. He squeezes my hand again. "Seriously, it's totally—"

"My mom's on her way," Ellie declares, coming back. She looks around the crowded lobby. "Where's Kyle?"

"Playing a video game," I say.

"Figures," she says, sounding disgusted. I want to ask her what's going on, but she sends me a message with her eyes that she doesn't want to talk about it in front of Brandon.

But Ellie's mom is driving all of us home, so I won't have a chance to talk to her until later. The four of us head outside and stand on the curb until Ellie's mom pulls up. The conversation is awkward, with Ellie and Kyle basically ignoring each other. When I see Ellie's mom come pulling into the parking lot, I'm relieved.

But then, right before we're supposed to hop in, I feel this weird brush of cold air, and I turn around, thinking that maybe it started snowing or something. But it isn't snow. It's Brandon's mom. And she hops into Ellie's mom's van right behind us.

Chapter

9

Okay, so this is awkward.

Here are the seating arrangements:

Ellie in the front seat with her mom.

Me in the middle section with Brandon.

Kyle in the backseat of the van, his legs stretched out in front of him, and Mrs. Dunham sitting on his legs.

She's a lot fainter than she usually is, which makes me think that she's having to put forth a tremendous amount of effort to even be here. It makes a chill slide down my spine, and I have that same thought again, that maybe she has something really important that she's trying to take care of. Is Brandon in some kind of danger? Is Grace? Why was she talking about a green paper? Would

Brandon know what that meant? Maybe I should ask him.

"How was the movie?" Mrs. Wilimena asks.

"Fine," Ellie says. She's staring out the window. Kyle coughs. What the heck is going on with those two?

"The green paper," Mrs. Dunham stage-whispers from the backseat. I force myself not to look at her. But it doesn't seem to make any difference. She just keeps whispering in this very creepy way.

After a few more minutes Mrs. Wilimena and Ellie start getting into a conversation about her cousin's wedding that's coming up, and Kyle pulls his iPod out of his pocket and sticks the buds into his ears. Mrs. Dunham is still whispering, but I'm starting to get a little more used to it. I'm able to tune her out, kind of like when you're trying to talk to someone on the phone and you can hear their TV in the background.

"So," I say to Brandon, trying to sound nonchalant, "what's your favorite color?"

"My favorite color?"

"Yeah," I say. That's one of the things you ask someone when you're trying to get to know them better, isn't it? "Mine's aqua. Or maybe purple."

"I guess mine would be orange," he says, like he's never thought of it.

"Really?" I ask. "Not green?"

"No," he says.

111

"Are you sure? Green is very pretty. Frogs are green."

"You like frogs?"

"No. I mean . . . Yeah, I guess . . . I don't know." This isn't going exactly according to plan. "I just meant that a lot of good things are green."

"Like frogs."

"Exactly."

"I like frogs," he says, "but my favorite animal is probably the jaguar."

Great. By the time we pull up in front of my house, I'm no closer to getting anything out of him than I was when we started.

"Well, bye," I say. "Thanks for the ride, Mrs. Wilimena. Ellie, text me later."

"I will," she says, and gives me a pointed look, like she can't wait to tell me what went down with her and Kyle.

I walk into my house, and Mrs. Dunham follows behind me.

But she must have expended too much energy while she was doing all that whispering, because even though she follows me up the stairs, by the time I get to my room, she's gone. I don't even have time to enjoy any of my ghost-free time, though, because Daniella takes over immediately. These spirits are really driving me crazy.

"Finally!" Daniella says. "I've been waiting for you all night."

"You were?"

"Yeah," she says, "and I have gossip." She moves her eyebrows up and down.

"What kind of gossip?" I ask warily. Anytime a ghost says they have gossip, it can't be a good thing.

"About Cindy," she says. "And your dad. She came over for dinner . . ."

"And they got into a big fight and he kicked her out of the house and said, 'Never come back here ever again'?" I ask hopefully, kicking my shoes off.

"No," she says. Daniella does a backbend and then a walkover until she's standing up. Wow. That's actually pretty impressive. I wonder how long it took her to learn that.

"Then, what?"

"She started asking him all these questions about your mom." Daniella sits down at my desk and waits for my reaction.

I'm at my dresser, taking my earrings out and putting my necklace back into my jewelry box, and my heart catches in my throat.

"Really?" I ask slowly. "What was she asking?"

"You know, like how long they were married, and why she left and stuff."

"And what did my dad say?"

"Just that your mom was always a free spirit, and that she just couldn't deal with the day-to-day stuff having to do with a family. He seemed really sad."

That's the thing that upsets me the most about my mom. Not even that she left me, because, like I said, I didn't even know her. It mostly upsets me that she left my dad. My dad loved her so much. He hasn't dated since she left.

"She was the love of his life," I tell Daniella.

"That's what he said," Daniella says. "Which Cindy *so* did not like. You could tell, even though she pretended that she was all sympathetic."

I sniff. "Ha!"

"I kind of like Cindy," Daniella says. She tilts her head to the side and thinks about it. "She's spunky."

"Figures."

"Anyway!" She jumps out of my desk chair and onto my bed. She lies on her stomach, her silky blond hair pooling around her shoulders. "Tell me what the plan is. You know, with Jen."

"Well, tomorrow's Saturday, so there's a gymnastics meet," I say. "I asked my dad to drive me so I can watch. I told him I'm thinking about joining the gymnastics team at school."

"Yay!" Daniella says. "And then, after the meet, you're going to ask her about the digging?"

114

"Ummm . . ." Is she crazy? I can't just bring up digging to Jen at her gymnastics meet. But something tells me I shouldn't tell Daniella that. "Well, I'm going to play it by ear," I say. "You know, take her lead."

Daniella looks doubtful, but before she can say anything else, I grab some soft pink pajama pants and a comfy gray tank top from my drawer and head to the bathroom to brush my teeth and get ready for bed.

So here's what went down with Ellie and Kyle during the movie:

The previews started, and Ellie was excited to be with him on the date, but she was already a little bit annoyed with him because he'd gotten cranky about where we were going to sit, and because I guess he was getting nacho crumbs all over the floor and on his shirt. So then she said, "Kyle, you look kind of a mess."

And then Kyle brushed his shirt off and said, "Better?"

And then Ellie was like, "Yeah." But then Kyle was crunching his chips too loud, and Ellie said, "Kyle, you might want to eat a little quieter."

And then Kyle was all, "Ellie, you might need to relax a little bit." And then they didn't talk to each other for the rest of the movie. I have to admit that when she tells me all this over text message, I'm a little disappointed. I expected something with much more drama.

Anyway, I tell Ellie that it wasn't really nice of her to say that Kyle looked like a mess, and then she says she said he looked "kind of" a mess, which I say is basically the same thing. But then she says that if he really cared about hanging out with her, he would have tried to do anything she asked, like eat like a normal person. And then *I* said she had a point, and that even though he might not do *anything* she asked, he could have at least tried to eat a little quieter, or maybe even just said, "I'm sorry, Ellie, but that really hurt my feelings. Next time you have a problem with my eating habits, maybe you could say it a little nicer" instead of just telling her to relax.

But of course most thirteen-year-old boys can't express themselves that way. Actually, most *people* can't express themselves that way. But when I tell Ellie this, she says Kyle could have at least tried, and even if he couldn't put his emotions into words, he shouldn't have just said that she needed to relax, because she thinks she's a very fun person, and not uptight at all. Which is sort of true. Ellie can be pretty relaxed about certain things, like how she went to the mall that day without even thinking about it, but sometimes she does get caught up in manners and etiquette and stuff.

But I don't say this, because she's my best friend, and of course I'm on her side.

Anyway, Ellie tells me all this over text message and it

takes us until, like, two in the morning for her to finally get it all out. We make plans to meet up for lunch the next day at this really cute café that's halfway between our houses so that we can discuss it more.

But first I have to get to the gymnastics meet in Cedar Falls. Which starts at nine a.m. Which means I have to be up by eight. On a Saturday. Which means I'm extremely cranky as I stumble down the stairs and into my dad's car. I told him I was meeting my friend Daniella there. Which isn't really a lie, since Daniella *is* going with me. Although I wouldn't exactly call her a friend, and I'm not meeting her there. She's riding over with us, ha-ha.

By the time we get to the meet, I'm still not fully awake. Thank God they have a concession stand. I buy a cup of coffee and something called "breakfast dough," which sounds gross but is actually this delicious warm fried dough dusted with powdered sugar and topped with strawberries and whipped cream.

We (well, I) find a seat way in the back of the gym, high up on the bleachers so that I can observe without anyone seeing me.

Both teams are warming up, flying over the mats, flipping all around, their legs and arms and ponytails in a whirl.

"Wow," I say to Daniella. "You used to do that?" I take a bite of breakfast dough. So. Good.

"Yeah," she says, looking longingly at the gymnasts.

"You miss it?"

"Yeah. Being part of a team, it was . . . it was fun." Her eyes start to fill up a little with tears. "It's hard," she says. "You know, remembering."

"Yeah," I say softly. I've seen this happen before, and it breaks my heart every single time. A ghost will start remembering their life, their old life, and the more they remember, the harder it gets for them. Add that to the fact that the longer they're around, the more they can handle, and so they don't even fade away when things get hard.

"Anyway," Daniella says, shaking her head and wiping away her tears. "What's our plan?"

"Why do you always need a plan?" I ask. "Don't you think it's better to just wing it?"

"No," she says. "'Failing to prepare is preparing to fail.'"

Wow. When did Daniella turn into some kind of self-help guru? "I guess," I say, "but—"

And then I stop. Oh. My. God. Oh my God, oh my God, oh my God. I do not believe it. Because right in front of me, through the double doors at the front of the gym, Brandon Dunham comes walking in.

He hasn't seen me yet, but I have to get out of here. I'll wait until he takes his seat, and then I can just quietly slip down the bleachers. I'll call my dad. He's probably not even that far away yet, and I'll tell him to come back, that I'm not feeling well, or better yet, that my friend never showed up and so I don't want to be here by myself. He'll think I'm so responsible that he'll—

Oh no. Grace is here! Grace is with them! It's Brandon and his dad and Grace, and she's dressed in her ninja or karate master or whatever-it-is costume, and what the *heck* are they doing here?

"What the heck are *they* doing here?" Daniella cries, annoyed. She floats down the bleachers a little bit, like maybe she's going to try to scare them away.

"My thoughts exactly," I say. "But don't worry. We'll just wait until they're sitting down, and then we'll sneak out. They'll never even see us."

"Sneak *out*?" Daniella says. "Oh, no, you don't. You're here to talk to Jen, and you are *going* to talk to Jen."

"Daniella," I say patiently. "I know this seems like a very big deal to you, moving on and everything. But you can't rush these things. And if you want to know the truth, it's not really my job to give up my whole entire—"

"KENDALL! OH MY GOD. LOOK, IT'S KENNNN-DALL. BRANDON'S GIRLFRIEND, KENDALL!" Grace's voice comes echoing through the gym, and since there aren't that many people here, it's loud, and everyone turns around to look.

How. Extremely. Embarrassing.

Brandon and his dad turn to look where Grace is pointing, which is, you know, right at me. (How did she even see me, anyway? She must have some kind of eagle vision.)

Brandon waves, looking surprised to see me. And then he, his dad, and Grace start CLIMBING THE BLEACHERS TOWARD ME.

"No!" Daniella yells. "No, no, no, no, no!" She stands up and stamps her foot at them and says, "Go away right now!" Wow. She's really regressing. I mean, she's kind of acting like a seven-year-old. And of course it doesn't matter because no one can hear her except for me.

"Hey," Brandon says as he gets closer. "What are you doing here?"

Good question. "Just, you know, came to watch the meet," I say. "I have a friend on the team. What are you doing here?"

"My cousin's on the team," he says.

"Our cousin COLLEEN," Grace reports. "She knows how to do ninja flips."

"I'll bet she does," I say, and give her a smile. "Well, I don't want to interrupt your family outing. So maybe we can catch up later?"

"You're not interrupting," Mr. Dunham says. He really is a nice guy. And then, before I can stop them, the Dunhams are all sitting down next to me. On the bleachers.

120

Even though I have, like, the worst seat ever. Seriously, you can hardly even see what's going on.

"These seats are stupid!" Grace yells. "I want to move down farther."

"Um, do you mind?" Mr. Dunham asks me and Brandon, looking a little embarrassed.

"Dad," Brandon says, "why don't you and Grace go and move down there, and I'll stay here with Kendall."

I feel a warm rush of excitement at the fact that he wants to be alone with me, but Daniella is scowling.

Once his dad and sister are gone, Brandon reaches over and takes my hand. His fingers intertwine with mine, just the way they did last night at the movie theater. I look at him, and for a second I think maybe he's going to kiss me, right there in the gym, so I quickly look away, because I'm not really sure if I'm ready for that.

"So which one is your friend?" he asks.

"That's her," I say as Jen goes tumbling by.

We watch the meet, and Brandon points out his cousin Colleen, who does really well. Cedar Falls wins the meet, but only by a couple of points, so the whole time, we're on the edge of our seats. Well, Brandon and I are. Daniella is down in the middle of the gym, practicing on all the equipment. It's actually quite distracting, and sometimes I kind of have a hard time following what's going on, since I keep watching her instead of the person who's competing.

At one point Brandon even asks me if maybe we should move a little closer to the action, since I might be having trouble seeing what's going on.

But the worst part is that after the whole thing is over, Brandon insists that we go back to meet his cousin. And when we get to the hall outside of the locker room, she comes out before I have a chance to make up some kind of excuse to get out of there. Jen's following behind her.

"Hey, Colleen," Brandon's dad says. "You did great."

"Thanks," she says, grinning.

Colleen, Mr. Dunham, and Grace move over to the side of the hallway and start chatting with Colleen's parents.

Jen looks at me. I look at Jen.

"Is this your friend?" Brandon asks.

I nod. Brandon waits for me to say something, which makes sense, because supposedly Jen is my friend, and friends, you know, talk. But I'm frozen, just standing there, not saying anything, mostly because I'm kind of afraid of what's going to happen. Is she going to accuse me of being a stalker? Is she going to freak out on me? Is she going to embarrass me in front of Brandon?

"Hey, Kendall," Jen says. Which is good. At least she's using my name. "Thanks for coming." And then she pushes past me and into the hallway that leads out of the school.

Brandon looks at me, confused. "I guess she didn't have time to talk."

"Well, we're not *that* good of friends," I say. "And besides, she's really busy."

Brandon nods, but I'm not sure he believes me. In fact, he probably thinks I'm some kind of loser who thinks she's friends with a high school gymnast when she's really not. I cover up for it by laughing and talking to Grace a little bit, but by the time my dad comes to pick me up, I'm feeling cranky.

When I get home, I'm still feeling all grouchy, so I head up to my room and pop a DVD into my player. It's time to get lost in some cheesy TV show, one of the ones where before you even start to watch it, you know everything's going to work out in the end.

I'm snuggling in under the covers and thinking maybe I'll take a nap before it's time to meet Ellie for lunch, since I was up so early and everything, when Daniella shows up.

"Go away," I say, pulling the covers over my head. "Seriously, I am so not in the mood." After the meet Daniella stayed behind so that she could practice some more on all the apparatus. Apparati? Apparatuses? Whatever. Anyway, she's probably here now to yell at me for not talking to Jen. And yeah, I guess I *am* a little behind when it comes to helping Daniella move on. But what was I supposed to do? Brandon and his father and his sister were there! Like

I could really say anything in front of them! They would have thought I was totally crazy.

"Kendall," Daniella says, and something about the tone of her voice makes me pull back the covers. I look at her face, which is pale, even for a ghost. "I think I did something horrible." She bites her lip.

"What do you mean?"

"I mean," she says, "that I did something horrible. When I was alive. I . . . I remember it." Her face is completely white now, and her blue eyes are like saucers.

I throw the covers off. There's only one place I can go to think when something this serious is happening, only one place where I do my best thinking. "We're going to the graveyard," I say.

We sit on my fave bench. I've got my red notebook and cell phone. (Just in case Brandon decides to call. This whole helping Daniella thing is important, but let's face it, I do have to pay attention to my love life. Plus I'm also waiting for Ellie to call me so that we can finalize our plans for lunch.)

"So what is it?" I ask. "What did you do that's so horrible?"

I have my pen poised over my notebook.

"You're going to write it *down*?" Daniella asks. She sounds panicked. She's next to me on the bench. She's not doing stretches or cartwheels or backbends or anything. It's kind of weird to see her still.

"Yes, I'm going to write it down."

"Why?"

"So I can remember all the details."

"But what if someone finds it?"

I sigh. "Daniella, if someone finds it, they're not going to be worried about whatever bad thing it is you did. If someone finds it, they're going to be worried about my mental health for writing down something a dead girl told me."

She cocks her head. "Good point."

"Okay, so . . ." I poise my pen again.

"I stole her boyfriend."

"Excuse me, what?"

"I stole Jen's boyfriend." Daniella looks down at the ground, and her eyes start to fill up with tears. "Travis, that kid from the mall? I didn't mean to. They had broken up, it was . . . it was kind of a gray area."

"What kind of a gray area?" I ask. Stealing someone's boyfriend seems pretty black and white to me.

"Well, she told me she didn't like him anymore. But I . . . I still knew it wasn't right, that I shouldn't have made a date with him."

I'm scribbling everything down, but I still don't understand. "So wait," I say. "You took her boyfriend? And what, you want to say you're sorry for it?"

"Yes."

I clap my hands. "And then you'll be able to move on!"

She doesn't look convinced. "You think?"

"Yes!" I say. "Definitely. A lot of times ghosts have to apologize to someone before they can move on." Yay, yay, yay! I'm so excited and in such a good mood that for a second I think maybe I'm even going to miss Daniella when she's gone. Yeah, she can be a pain, but at least she's been keeping things interesting.

But my good mood doesn't last long. Because at that moment, for the second time that day, Brandon Dunham shows up at the same place I am.

Chapter

10

"**Hey,**" **he says, shielding** his eyes from the sun as he walks up the tree-lined path toward where I'm sitting. He smiles. "Fancy seeing you here."

"Yeah," I say, smiling back. "Are you following me, Brandon Dunham?"

"Maybe *you're* following *me*."

"But I got here first."

"Good point." He sits down next to me on the bench. Daniella rolls her eyes and then scoots over. "What are you doing here?" Brandon asks.

Good question. I try to come up with a reason I'd be sitting in a cemetery. Which, let's face it, *is* kind of weird.

"What are *you* doing here?" I shoot back. I hope he hasn't heard me talking to myself. How humiliating.

"I came to visit my mom's grave," he says.

Oh. Right. That makes sense. I'm surprised I haven't seen him here before. "I came to visit . . . my grandma's grave." I'm sitting in front of her grave, so it's not even really that much of a lie. And it makes perfect sense.

"Ugh," Daniella says. "I really cannot take another episode of *As the Middle School Drama Turns*." Which is both (a) mean and (b) not that funny, but I forgive her since I'm so close to getting rid of her. Plus after she says it, she goes away, which is a huge relief.

"Is this your grandma's grave?" Brandon asks, gesturing toward the gravesite.

"Yes."

He nods, then takes a flower out of the bouquet he's holding and sets it down on her stone.

"Thanks," I say. "That was really sweet."

"No problem," he says. "Do you want to come with me to my mom's grave?" He looks down at the ground shyly.

"I'd be happy to," I say.

We walk through the cemetery over to the grave. It's a beautiful black marble headstone, and Brandon sets down the rest of the flowers in front of it. And after Brandon has a private moment at his mom's stone, I ask him if he's okay.

"Yeah," he says as we start walking down the path and

toward the front of the cemetery. "The weird thing is, when I leave her grave, a lot of times it makes me feel better, you know? It's like I know she would want me to be happy."

"Yeah." And I know it's an emotional moment and all, but I can't stop thinking about Mrs. Dunham freaking out about that green paper. I clear my throat. "Sooo . . . ," I say, running my hand along the branches of a hydrangea bush as we walk by. "What was your mom like?"

"What was she like?"

"Yeah, like, was she, you know, strict?" I make my voice sound sympathetic and get ready to listen about all the ridiculous over-the-top rules Mrs. Dunham made Brandon follow.

"Not really."

"She wasn't?" I'm shocked. I guess being dead is making Mrs. Dunham really cranky.

"You seem surprised."

"No," I say. "I just, um . . . What was her favorite color?"

Brandon laughs and tips his head back. The sunlight glints off his hair. I knew he was the type to have sunlight glinting off his hair! Why is it boys are always the ones with the best natural highlights? So not fair. "What's with you and colors?" he asks.

"What do you mean?"

"Well, you were asking me what my favorite color was last night."

"Oh. Well, I just think that your favorite color says a lot about you as a person." I wonder if telling him it's because I'm interested in fashion design or something would be going too far, and then decide it probably would. I mean, I already lied to him about being interested in gymnastics. How many fake interests can one girl have?

"My mom's favorite color was purple," he says.

Crap. "Well, I'm thinking of changing my favorite color to green." This is a complete fabrication. I actually kind of hate green.

"Green's good for a favorite color," Brandon says. He sounds distracted, like he's not really paying attention. Not that I can blame him. I mean, it's not the most fascinating topic, and besides, we pretty much had this exact same conversation in the car on the way home from the movie. But it's not like I can just *ask* him about the green paper. He would think I was completely and totally out of my mind.

"Do you have any favorite things that are green?" I ask, in a last-ditch effort to get some info out of him.

"I don't know," he says. "Maybe grass? Oh, look, there's my dad." He points over to where his dad's car is parked at the end of the road. "See you later, Kendall."

"Bye," I say weakly. It's only when he's gone that I realize he didn't say he would text me later or anything. And he didn't try to hold my hand once.

• • •

"My life sucks," I whine an hour later when I'm cozied up in a booth at the Garden Café across from Ellie.

"Mine too," Ellie says morosely. "Like, I thought I liked Kyle, but it turns out he's just a big weirdo."

"Why, did he do something else?" I ask. I take a big bite of my cranberry scone and look warily over to the other side of the room, where Mrs. Dunham is sitting at a corner table and sort of . . . glaring at me. I'm pretty afraid of her, if you want to know the truth. She's looking crankier than usual. Which probably means that she really, really wants me to do something. And something tells me I'd better figure out what it is. And fast.

"Yes," Ellie says. "Look." She shoves her phone across the table at me, and I look at it. A text from Kyle. *Sry abt last night*, it says. *I want to make it up 2 u! another date?*

"What's wrong with that?" I ask. "At least he's apologizing." I check my own phone, but of course there's still no text from Brandon. Not that I expected one so soon after we left each other, but still. I'm feeling very melancholy. I'm a little closer to getting rid of Danielle, but I still have no idea what Mrs. Dunham wants. It's so upsetting that I'm wearing my hair plain and down. And I never wear it plain and down.

"I don't know," Ellie says. She frowns into her apple walnut salad.

"Ohmigod," I say, realizing now what this is about. "You like him! You, like, *really* like him."

"No, I don't!"

"Ellie," I say, "you've had a crush on him for more than two days. That means you really, really like him. You *like him* like him."

"That's way too many 'likes' to make sense." But she blushes, letting me know that I'm right. "Anyway," she says, "I do think you're right that I'm being way too hard on him." She takes a sip of her boysenberry iced tea. "And you're also right that it wasn't that nice of me to say that he looked a mess."

"No," I agree, "it wasn't."

"So, what's going on with you?" she asks.

"Nothing." I fill her in on what happened today, as much as I can without revealing the stuff about Daniella and Mrs. Dunham. Not for the first time, I think about what would happen if I just told Ellie about seeing ghosts. But I know it's too big of a risk. I'd be totally heartbroken if it messed up our friendship.

"Don't worry so much," she says. "Brandon likes you. And if he can't see how amazing you are, then he's not the guy for you."

I rip off another piece of scone. "I just wish this whole liking-boys thing wasn't so complicated. Remember how easy it used to be when we didn't ever go out on dates?"

"Yes." Ellie sighs. It seems like it was forever ago, even though it's really only been a few days.

We spend the next hour talking and laughing, and by the time I leave, I'm feeling a little bit better. I mean, there's nothing to be nervous about. Everything is going to work out. With me, with Brandon, with Daniella, even with Mrs. Dunham. I'm convinced of it, especially when she disappears in the middle of lunch and doesn't come back.

And that night I sleep better than I have in days.

But by the time lunch rolls around on Monday, I haven't heard from Brandon at all. No texts, no phone calls, nothing. He even rushed into math and then rushed out, and he hardly even said anything to me except for "Hi" and "Bye." We had a test, and so we didn't have a chance to talk. Although the good thing is that I think I actually might have done okay on the test. Since I had nothing to do yesterday, Daniella quizzed me on all my equations. She's actually very good at math. Who knew she could be so helpful?

Of course, the one time I do well, Mr. Jacobi announces that we're not going to be grading our papers in class. Apparently there's been some kind of scandal with kids announcing the wrong grade and adding points on top of what they were really supposed to have. Mr. Jacobi seems shocked that anyone would do this, even though you'd have to be kind of stupid to trust a bunch of seventh graders to be honest about their grades.

"Kyle and I are a couple!" Ellie squeals at lunch as she

sits down next to me, her tray clattering onto the table. A piece of pineapple from her fruit cocktail flies off and onto the bench next to her.

"Ohmigod," I say. "Are you serious?"

"Yes," she says, blushing. "We decided this morning, after I apologized for what I said to him and accepted his apology for being so weird at the movies."

"Ellie! Your first boyfriend! Holy crap, this is major. We have to—"

But before I can say anything, Kyle comes over to our table and sits down next to us. Oh. Right. Now that he's Ellie's boyfriend, I guess he's going to be sitting with us at lunch. And then Brandon comes and sits down next to him! Okay. Don't panic. Of course Brandon is going to sit here. Kyle's his best friend, and so of course they're going to sit together. *Just be cool,* I tell myself. No need to get all nervous.

"So that was fun on Saturday," I blurt. Oh, God. Way to be cool, Kendall.

"What happened on Saturday?" Kyle asks. He reaches over and pulls a tater tot off Ellie's tray and pops it into his mouth.

"Nothing," I say. "We just kept running into each other, that's all."

"Where?" Kyle asks.

"At the gymnastics meet," Brandon says.

"What gymnastics meet?" Ellie asks. "You never told me anything about a gymnastics meet."

Oh, God. "It was nothing," I say. "I just went to go and see my friend Jen in her meet."

"Jen who?"

"Ummm . . ." I rack my brains, trying to remember Jen's last name. Do I even know her last name? "Smith." It's the first thing that pops into my head, because it's the most common last name in the United States. So I have the most statistical chance of being right.

"Jen Smith?" Ellie asks, frowning. "Never heard of her."

"Um, Brandon?" I ask quickly. "You wanna come with me to get some juice?"

"But you have chocolate milk," Ellie says.

"I know," I say, "but I want some juice." I turn back to Brandon. "Will you come with me?" I need to get him away from Ellie before she starts asking me all kinds of questions that make it clear that I don't know Jen at all, and have never shown any kind of interest in gymnastics.

"Sure," Brandon says.

"So how'd you do on the test?" I ask Brandon once we're in the lunch line. The long lunch line. The long lunch line we now have to wait in so that I can grab a juice. A juice I don't even want.

"I think I did okay," he says. "How about you?" He's being modest, of course. He probably got a hundred.

135

"I think I did well, actually," I say. "I kind of wish we'd gotten to grade them in class."

"Mr. Jacobi probably knew you did well, and so that's why he collected them," Brandon says, teasing. "He probably made up that whole thing about people giving the wrong grades."

"Probably," I say, grinning. "I'm, like, his arch-nemesis."

"I wonder why."

"Well," I say, grabbing a can of cranberry-grape juice as the line moves forward, "I'm always hanging out in the English office, and he doesn't like that."

"Why?"

"Why am I always hanging out there, or why doesn't he like it?"

"Both."

"I'm hanging out there because I know Mrs. D'Amico, the head of the English department. She was my grandmother's best friend before she died." Brandon squeezes my shoulder and gives me a smile when my grandma comes up. I really like that. Not just because the shoulder squeeze is sending bursts of electricity through my body, but because most people would give you a sympathetic look when you bring up someone close to you that died. But Brandon smiled, like, *Wow, that's really great that you have someone to remember your grandmother with.* "And my theory is that Mr. Jacobi doesn't like it because he likes

Ms. Benson, the new English teacher. Her office is next to Mrs. D'Amico's, and I don't think Mr. Jacobi wants students seeing him hanging out there."

"He likes *Ms. Benson*?" Brandon asks.

"Oops." I clap my hand over my mouth. But I'm grinning. "It's just a theory! Although I did see them flirting in the hall."

Brandon grins back. *See?* I tell myself. *There's nothing to be nervous about.* Brandon has no idea that I don't really know Jen, or that anything was amiss this weekend. I'm totally working myself up over nothing.

Everything's fine. All I have to do is just try to keep everything having to do with these stupid ghosts to myself. I haven't even seen Mrs. Dunham for a couple of days, and even if she *does* come back, there's no rule saying that I *have* to help her. At the very least, she's going to have to give me some more info about what she's talking about. Or at least stop being so confrontational.

But then I see something. Something that kind of throws the whole plan about forgetting about the ghost stuff out the window. And that's a piece of green paper, sticking out of Brandon's book bag.

So here's the thing. I try to ignore it. I really do. That stupid piece of green paper, I really, really, really try to just pretend I didn't see it. But the problem is that it's just . . . *there.*

All day. I don't know why I never noticed it before. Because now it's taunting me. Every time I see Brandon, it's peeking out of his bag. Seriously. Every. Single. Time. If the paper's so important that his dead mom is haunting me because of it, you'd think he'd take better care of it. I mean, really. I want to ask him what's on it, but the one time he catches me looking at it, at the end of the day, he looks all flustered and then quickly pushes it back into his bag.

I'm in a horrible mood by the time school lets out, and it's not helped by the fact that now I have to head over to the high school to have another run-in with Jen and tell her the info about Daniella stealing her boyfriend.

"You'll be able to convince her to talk to you now, though," Daniella says. "Since you have personal information about her. Oh, and don't forget to tell her about the digging."

"Okay," I say, not wanting to burst her bubble by reminding her that Jen hates me. "I'll tell her about the digging." Not.

"This is so great!" She's cartwheeling all down the street as we walk to the high school. It could definitely be my imagination, but I think some of the drivers passing by are looking at me strange, thinking that I'm talking to myself. But obviously I don't have time to think about that right now. I mean, I have much bigger issues. "When will I get to leave?" Daniella asks. "Once you tell her that I'm sorry for stealing her boyfriend, then do you think that I'll just, like, pop away?" Her face is all excited. "Where will I go? I hope it doesn't hurt." She thinks about it. "Although, on the other hand, no pain, no gain, so . . ."

"I'm sure it'll be fine," I say, which is, of course, a complete lie. I have no idea how any of this is going to go. But whatever. I'm all about trying to make her feel better. I mean, at least one of us should be happy.

When we get to the school, the gymnastics team is finishing up their practice, and there are a few parents and some other kids sort of milling around, so I walk into the gym and take a seat in the bleachers. I guess they must let people in to watch once parents start arriving to pick up their kids. Of course, I'm not here to pick anyone up. But whatevs. I could totally be someone's sister or something.

Jen spots me across the gym, and I look away so that she doesn't get too weirded out. But out of the corner of my eye I see one of her friends pointing at me and whispering.

Great. Now I'm getting a reputation. A reputation as a scary stalker girl.

"It's okay," Daniella says when she sees them staring at me. "I'll be gone in a couple hours, and then you won't even have to deal with this anymore."

"Thanks," I say. I don't think this is going to be as easy as she thinks, but I'm surprised to realize that I actually *will* miss her when she's gone. Yeah, she's been annoying, but she hasn't been that bad—as far as ghosts go, anyway. And she did give me some very fab ideas for how to do my hair. And besides, once she's gone, who knows who's going to show up? It might be Brandon's mom.

"Hey, Kendall!" Someone calls my name, and I look up to see Jen standing at the bottom of the bleachers, waving up at me.

"Yay!" Daniella says. "Look, she likes you now! Now let's get this over with." She cartwheels down the bleachers and onto the gym floor.

"Hi," I say, looking at Jen and pretending like I'm not there to stalk her. "You looked really great out there. Your back somersaults were amazing." This, at least, is true. I've totally been reading up on gymnastics and working on getting the lingo down.

"Thanks." She looks down and pushes the toe of her sneaker into the gym floor. "Listen, can I talk to you for a second?"

I'm surprised. And a little nervous. Is she going to threaten to get a restraining order or something? My dad would so not like that. I'd definitely be grounded. How would I explain that one to Brandon? "Sorry, Brandon. I can't hang out for a while. I'm grounded for stalking that girl from the gymnastics meet."

"Sure," I tell Jen. I take a deep breath, then get up and follow her out into the hall, around the corner, and into

140

the locker room. It's empty, I guess because the gymnastics team has their own separate sports locker room. This one must just be used for gym class. And it smells like it too. Eww.

"So listen," Jen says, sighing and pushing her hair back from her face. "I don't want to be rude or anything, because I'm sure you're a very nice girl. But you're starting to freak me out a little bit."

"What do you mean?" I wrinkle up my forehead and cock my head to the side, like I'm confused. I'm trying to look innocent, but of course I know what she means. That I'm, like, her stalker. No, not *like* her stalker. I pretty much *am* her stalker.

"I mean you keep showing up at all my gymnastics stuff. And I did some research on you, and I found out that you don't even *do* gymnastics."

"You checked up on me?" I exclaim.

"Yeah." She plops her bag down onto one of the benches, and then pulls out a hoodie. She slides her arms into it and then zips it up. "You're not the only one that can find out things about people, you know. Google and Facebook are available to everyone."

Crap. I knew I should have set my Facebook page to private.

Daniella, who is now apparently starting to realize that things aren't going to go as smoothly as she hoped, starts to have a meltdown. "Tell her you *are* into gymnastics!" she says. "I'll help you! Go on, tell her you like to vault. I'll feed you the information!"

But I know this won't help. It's time to come clean.

"Jen," I say, "I'm sorry if I've freaked you out in any way. The thing is, you're right. I'm not a gymnast."

"What are you *doing*?" Daniella yells. She tries to slap me on the back, but of course her arm just goes floating right through me. "Don't tell her that! She's not going to believe anything you say now."

"Then what are you doing?" Jen asks, picking up her bag and slinging it over her shoulder. Her eyes dart to the door, like she's making sure she has a clear path in case she needs to escape. "Why are you obsessed with Daniella?"

"I'm not." I take a deep breath. "Daniella and I were friends."

Jen looks at me incredulously. "You were friends?"

"Yes," I say, "and I . . . I wanted to come and tell you something that I thought Daniella would want you to know."

"You're lying!" Daniella shrieks. "We weren't friends. God, if you were going to just lie anyway, you should have kept going with the thing about you being a gymnast." She thinks about it. "Although, this could work." She nods. "Go on." I resist the urge to roll my eyes.

"Like what?" Jen asks. Her face is kind of turning now

from being scared to being a little . . . nervous. Almost like she knows what's coming.

"Like she wanted you to know that she's sorry for stealing Travis from you."

Jen's face goes white, and she drops her bag onto the floor. "How did you know about that?"

"I told you," I say, "we were friends."

"And she *told* you that?"

"Yes," I say. "She was really upset about it. She, um, wished it had never happened." This, at least, isn't a lie.

"It's true," Daniella says to Jen. "I shouldn't have done that. I'm so, so, so sorry." Her voice, just a second ago screechy and annoying, is now soft and apologetic.

"She didn't really steal him," Jen says, chewing on her lip. "She . . . I mean, she . . ." She sighs, then shakes her head and starts over. "She didn't really take him. We had broken up." She looks down at her hands. "It was kind of a gray area, I guess."

"Not really," Daniella whispers, even though she told me before that it *was* a gray area. "I knew she still liked him."

"Well, she felt really bad," I say.

"Why did she tell you about it?" Jen asks. She's looking at me, her green eyes serious.

"Why did she tell me about it?" Good question.

"Yeah. I mean, no offense, but you're in middle school. I doubt you would have a ton of advice for her about boys."

At first I'm kind of insulted, because hello, I have a kind of, sort of boyfriend. I wonder if I should tell her this. But then I realize she's obviously right, and that I'd be totally out of my element when it comes to this stuff. Not to mention that my kind of, sort of boyfriend's mom keeps showing up and, like, haunting me, and I'm so nervous he's going to think I'm a crazy person that I can never relax. I'm definitely not really on the right track when it comes to dating.

I look at Daniella for help, but she just shrugs her shoulders. Great.

"I don't know why she told me," I say. "Um, maybe she figured it was safe? She knew that I didn't know anyone she knew, so it wasn't like I could tell anyone, you know?"

"Yeah," Jen says. For a second I think she's going to believe me. She looks down at the floor, thinking. But then she looks back up and says, "How did you know Daniella?"

"How did I know her?"

"Yeah, like how did you guys meet?"

"Umm . . ." I try to remember if I ever told her how I knew Daniella, but then I realize that of course I didn't, since up until a few minutes ago, I was still pretending Daniella and I were strangers. "Our families were really close," I decide.

"Funny," Jen says. "We were best friends for a long time, and she never mentioned you. And I don't remember seeing you at the funeral."

Uh-oh. "I didn't go to the funeral," I say. "My, uh, parents thought I was too young to see something so traumatic." Totally plausible!

"Right." She picks her bag up and hefts it over her shoulder. "Look, whatever happened between me and Daniella, it . . . it doesn't matter anymore. And honestly, it's really upsetting to talk about it. So I'd appreciate it if you just left me alone." She starts walking toward the door. She's leaving!

"Wait!" I yell desperately. "Daniella was always talking to me about some kind of digging. Do you know anything about that?"

"I have no idea what you're talking about," she yells over her shoulder. "But I'm going to tell my mom about you. And if you show up here again, I'm going to call the police." And then she walks out.

"Why am I still here?" Daniella demands, looking down at herself. "You told her I was sorry, so WHY. AM. I. STILL. HERE?"

I sigh. "Either she didn't believe me," I say, sitting down on the bench and putting my head in my hands, "or there's a lot more to the story."

Chapter

11

Well. I guess that didn't go very well. I mean, anytime someone threatens to call law enforcement on you, it's definitely not good. Not to mention that I thought I had the mystery all figured out, only to find out I have more work to do. I'm so upset that when I get home, I take a shower and then spend two hours putting my hair into a million little braids. It takes forever, but with my hands occupied, my mind has a chance to calm down.

"Let's eat out tonight," I say to my dad at dinnertime. "I feel like getting out of the house." The weather has been getting a little colder lately, and before we know it, it's going to be winter, and then I'll never get out of here. My dad, even though he's this big, burly guy, likes to hibernate in the winter, spending most of his time reading books in front of the fireplace or playing games on his iPad. He hates the snow.

"Sounds good," he says.

So we go to the Château, my fave Italian restaurant, which has the yummiest chicken Alfredo. We order cheesy garlic bread and talk about my dad's work and how I'm doing better in math, and it's actually a really nice time, just what I need to distract myself from all the ghost and boy drama that's been going on.

We even get tiramisu for dessert, but then, just as I'm thinking of ordering another Shirley Temple, a voice rings out over the dining room.

"Bob! And Kennnddalll! What a surprise!" I turn around to see Cindy Pollack barreling toward us. And okay, she's not really barreling, because hello, she's tiny. But anytime I see Cindy, it really does look like she's barreling, because I don't want her anywhere near me.

"Hi, Cindy," my dad says. He shoots me a look over the table. A look that says to be nice.

"Hi, Cindy," I say politely. I wonder if she's now switched over to full-blown stalker mode. I mean, there's no way she could have known we were here, since it was a totally last-minute thing. But maybe she was waiting outside our house, just sitting there in her car, waiting to follow us if we went somewhere. Things like that really do happen. Ellie's dad is a psychiatrist, and one time one of his patients totally started stalking him and would even go through his trash when they put it out on the curb. My dad should really stop leading Cindy on. She's so obviously in love with him. "We were just finishing up," I say pointedly, but she doesn't get the hint.

"Oooh, tiramisu," she says. "I love tiramisu."

"Me too," I say. "I always eat the whole piece. By myself."

"Would you like to join us?" my dad asks.

"I don't want to intrude," Cindy says as she sits down. Which is ridiculous, because if she didn't want to intrude, she could have just left. Which means that she *did* want to intrude and was just saying that she didn't.

She reaches over and grabs a fork off the table (why didn't the waitress clear those extra place settings when we sat down? Her tip is so going down) and then takes a bite of our dessert.

"Yum," Cindy says. I sigh. "So, Kendall," she continues, "how was your date the other night?"

"It was good," I say, thawing a little bit because it was nice of her to remember. And also because it was her idea to let me go, and if she'd said no, who knows what my dad would have said?

"So who is this boy?"

"His name's Brandon," I say, my face getting all red.

"Is it serious?"

On the other side of the booth, my dad shifts and looks uncomfortable. "It's not serious," he says. "They're only in seventh grade."

What's that supposed to mean? That just because I'm young, I can't be in love? I mean, I'm not in love with Brandon, but still. I don't want to think that the thing with Brandon doesn't mean anything.

"Things are going great," I say. It's a halfway lie, of course. Things are going sort of great. Besides the fact that his mom keeps showing up. And that I spotted that green paper in his backpack. And that even though Ellie and Kyle are boyfriend-girlfriend, Brandon and I are nowhere near being official.

"They are?" My dad seems surprised.

"Yeah," I say, taking some more tiramisu. "Why do you seem surprised?" Aren't your parents supposed to think that every boy should be in love with you? My dad should be thinking I'm so fabulous that of course Brandon would fall in love with me, not questioning the validity of my relationship. Although, obviously it's not really a relationship. It's just . . . I don't know what it is.

"I'm not surprised," he says. "Any boy would be lucky to have you." That's more like it.

"Well, I think it's wonderful," Cindy says. She reaches over and forks up the last piece of tiramisu. "Is he cute?"

"He's very cute," I say. "He has floppy hair and a perfect smile. Do you remember him from the mall?"

149

"Sort of," she says.

My dad shifts in the booth again. "Well," he says, "I think it's time I met this Brandon."

"What?" I almost shriek. Is he crazy? I can't have my dad meeting Brandon. Talk about a disaster waiting to happen. "No! And besides, you already met him, remember?"

"When?" My dad shifts in his seat and looks suspicious, like I'm trying to get one over on him by making him think he met Brandon when he didn't.

"At the mall that day." I decide it's time to change the subject. "Cindy, I really like your sweater. Where did you get it?"

"I made it myself," she says. "In the beading class I'm taking."

"Really?" Wow. That's actually pretty impressive. It's this cool V-neck black sweater with rainbow glitter beads that sparkle in the light.

"Kendall, I'm serious," my dad says, obviously not ready to let it go. "If you're going to be spending time with this boy, I think it's time I met him." He puffs out his chest, like he needs to protect me or something. I want to tell him this isn't the Middle Ages, but something tells me that won't go over so well.

"I'm not going to be spending time with him," I say. "I mean, I am, but I'm not . . . It's not . . . You don't have to meet him."

"I'm sure Kendall's smart enough to know if you'd approve of the boy she's dating," Cindy says, I guess in an effort to save me. I throw her a grateful smile.

"I'm sure she is too," my dad says. "Which is why she shouldn't have a problem inviting him over for dinner."

"For *dinner*?"

"Yes. This weekend. And until then, I don't think you should be hanging out with him."

"*What?*" Cindy and I say at the same time.

"Bob," Cindy says, her voice gentle, "don't you think that's a little harsh?"

"No," my dad says. And that's that. My dad might ask Cindy for advice, but once he's made up his mind about something, there's nothing you can do to change it.

"How am I going to get Brandon to come over to my house for dinner?" I whine to Ellie later that night. I'm at her house, helping her organize her wardrobe. Ellie's not a morning person, and lately she's been almost missing the bus every single day because she's obsessing over what to wear. So we're going to coordinate her outfits for the week, including applicable shoes and accessories, and lay them out ahead of time.

"Just ask him," Ellie says, and shrugs. Easy for her to say. She has a boyfriend.

"I can't just ask him! He'll think I'm, like, obsessed with him or something."

"Aren't you?"

"Nooo!" I think about it. "Well, okay, maybe a little. But I don't want *him* to know that."

Ellie picks up a yellow dress that's lying in a ball on her bedroom floor. "What do you think of this dress?" She holds it up in front of her and poses in front of the silver full-length mirror that's hanging on the back of her door.

"It's cute," I say, "but it's a summer dress."

"But," she says, "if I put some black tights under it and pair it with a cute sweater, it would be fab."

"Totally," I say. "But it needs to be washed."

Ellie nods and then throws it into the needs-to-be-washed pile that's rapidly growing on her floor. "When was the last time you did laundry?" I ask her. Ellie looks at me blankly, like the thought of doing laundry is crazy. "You do do laundry, don't you?"

"Of course!"

"Ellie?"

"Well . . . I mean, my mom does it."

"When was the last time your mom decided to do laundry? Because most of your stuff is dirty. No wonder you have a hard time picking out what to wear in the morning."

"Well, she'll do it whenever I need it, but . . . I just . . . sometimes I forget to bring it down to the laundry room."

She holds up a beaded blue shirt that hits just above her knees.

"So cute with white leggings," I tell her. She tosses it into the pile of needs-to-be-washed. I throw myself down onto her bed and look up at the ceiling. "Oooh," I moan. "What am I going to do?"

"Call him," Ellie says. Her words are muffled because she's in her closet now, poking around. When she emerges, she has a huge pile of clothes in her arms that's threatening to spill over and fall onto the floor.

"And say what?"

"Invite him over," she says. And then she drops the clothes. "Actually, invite us all over!"

"What do you mean?"

"Me, Kyle, you, and Brandon," she says. "That way it'll seem more like a party. And your dad won't have a chance to grill him too hard with everyone there."

"That's a great idea!" I say, sitting up. "Ellie, you're a total genius!" I step around all the piles of clothes that are on her floor and start picking through them. "And now you need to let me borrow something to wear."

It's actually relatively easy to convince my dad that he should let me have three people over instead of just one. My dad loves Ellie.

Daniella, however, is not happy. Not one little bit.

"You can't just have them over tonight!" she yells at me on Saturday. We're walking through the cemetery because she insisted that we talk, and I couldn't have a whole conversation with her with my dad around.

"Yes, I can," I tell her. "Why wouldn't I be able to have them over? They're my friends. And besides, my dad is starting to freak out about the whole Brandon thing, and I have to make him feel better." It's a little chilly out, and I walk faster, hoping it will warm me up. I really should be at home, getting ready for my big night. But no.

"But what about meeeee?" Daniella whines, and then starts walking on her hands. God, what a show-off.

"Well, you can come too, of course," I say. Although I'm just saying it to be nice. I know I said I would miss her when she's gone, and I will, but I don't really want her at dinner. Who knows what kind of trouble she'll cause?

"I don't want to come!" she says. "I'm on the verge of some kind of breakthrough. And I think that, as my ghost protector, you should be helping me to get through it, not planning dates."

"What kind of breakthrough?" I ask.

"I'm not sure." She bites her lip and tosses her long blond hair over her shoulder. "But I know it's coming. I'm remembering something about that digging." She frowns, her pretty face crumpling up in concentration.

"So I'm supposed to cancel my date with the most perfect boy to ever live because you might remember something about digging? Yeah, I don't think so." I'm at my favorite bench now, and so I plop down onto it and raise my face toward the sky. The sun is peeking out now, even though it's chilly. It's the first sunny day in a long time, and I feel my spirits start to pick up.

Tonight is going to be great, I tell myself. I mean, how could it not be? Brandon immediately accepted my invite to hang out when I asked him over, he's been really friendly and flirty with me lately, I haven't said anything weird or crazy to him, his mom hasn't been around at all, and—

Wait. Is that . . . Oh, God. It is! It's Brandon's mom. She's lurking by some headstones! I've totally jinxed it by thinking about how she hasn't been around lately! Why is she showing up at the graveyard? It's like she wants to know where she ended up. Which is really silly, when you think about it, because she *knows* where she ended up. At the cemetery, which is where everyone ends up. Although, I guess some people get cremated. I don't know if I've ever met a ghost that was cremated. I never really ask them. But maybe I should start. Because what if getting cremated means that you can't come back? Not that I want to come back, but if I ever had unfinished business, then—

Oh, God. Mrs. Dunham spots me and then starts stomping over toward the bench I'm sitting on.

"Who's that?" Daniella asks.

"That's Mrs. Dunham," I say warily.

"Brandon's mom?"

"Yes," I say. "She's a ghost."

"She's a ghost? Like me?" Daniella starts getting excited. But something tells me Mrs. Dunham isn't going to be all that excited to talk to Daniella.

"The green paper," Mrs. Dunham says. She shakes her finger at me and then gets really close. "You need to put your name on THAT. GREEN. PAPER." Her eyes feel like they're boring into mine, and even though they're normally blue, today they look gray and not friendly at all. "I mean it, Kendall," she says.

"Wow, lady," Daniella says, "you need to back off." I guess it's easy not to be scared of a ghost when you are one yourself. For the first time, I'm glad Daniella's here. Maybe if Mrs. Dunham starts with me, Daniella will protect me. I mean, she's pretty muscular.

But Mrs. Dunham doesn't seem intimidated. She keeps glaring at me.

"Ewww," Daniella says. "What's her problem?"

"That's the thing," I say, and sigh. "I have no idea. Come on," I say to Daniella. I turn and start walking back toward my house. I wait until I'm almost home before I turn around to check for Mrs. Dunham. But she's gone.

. . .

156

When I get inside, my dad's in the kitchen, flipping through a cookbook. And then he announces that he's making pot roast for the dinner with my friends tonight.

"We can't have pot roast!" I say. I go over to the cookbook and flip the pages, looking for something a little more fun. Why is my dad using a cookbook, anyway? Everyone knows you can get way better recipes on the internet. How old school.

"Why can't we have pot roast?" He's over by the stove now, and he pulls this big roast out of the oven, bastes it, and then slides it back in. Then he starts lining up cans of vegetables on the counter.

"Because you can't . . ." I wonder how I'm going to explain this to him, and then realize that it's probably pointless. "Dad, we need to, like, order pizza or have tacos or something."

"Order pizza? But I'm a great cook!" He turns back to the cookbook and flips it back to the pot roast recipe.

"Ellie's a vegetarian," I try.

He points to a package that's sitting on the counter. "I'm making her a veggie burger."

"Yeah, but . . . Dad, this has to be fun." I imagine all of us sitting around the table, eating pot roast and having stilted conversation. I mean, I'm sure the pot roast will be good and everything, but I'm trying to make this a fun, normal night, not a night filled with pot roast and vegetables. That doesn't say "party." That says "family dinner where my dad is going to interrogate Brandon and everyone is going to have the worst time ever."

The doorbell rings, and my heart drops to my shoes. "That can't be them already, can it?" I haven't even put on my dinner outfit (black ballet flats, black tiered poofy skirt, white long-sleeved shirt with little hearts all over) or done my hair (straightened and curled at the bottoms, but with a string of tiny heart jewels woven through it).

"Uh, no," my dad says. He wipes his hands on one of the dishcloths that's sitting on the counter, and looks guilty. "That's probably Cindy."

"Cindy! Why is Cindy here?"

"I thought it would be good for her to meet Brandon," my dad says.

I narrow my eyes at him. This is turning out to be a very, very bad idea. Now not only are Kyle and Ellie coming (which at first seemed like a good idea because it would be more of a party, but now I'm not so sure), but we are having pot roast and Cindy is coming. Which is okay, because Cindy will probably like Brandon and say something to my dad, but it's not really her place. She's not my mother. She's not even my stepmother. She's not even my dad's girlfriend! I mean, talk about trying to weasel your way into the family. I know I keep saying that, but come on! It's true! I might need to have a talk with my dad about this. I really do not need a female role model.

"Do you want to go and get the door?" my dad asks. He's opening a can of corn.

"Not really," I grumble. But I get up from the table and go to the door.

"Hello!" Cindy says when I open it. "Don't you look adorable!"

I raise my eyebrows and look down at what I'm wearing. Black pajama pants, a long-sleeved white T-shirt, and a gray and pink hoodie. "I haven't gotten ready yet," I say. And then I add pointedly, "No one's coming for another couple of hours."

She's oblivious to the fact that she's super-early, and breezes by me and into the kitchen.

"Kendall," my dad says, "you could offer to take Cindy's coat."

"Can I take your coat, Cindy?" I ask, sighing.

She slides it off and hands it to me. I hang it up in the hall closet, then return to the kitchen. "Cindy," I say, "how do you feel about pot roast?"

"Oh, I love pot roast," she says, and then she giggles. Seriously. She totally giggles. She's kind of too old to be giggling, but whatever. "Your dad makes the best pot roast."

"When have you ever had my dad's pot roast?" I ask.

My dad clears his throat and starts getting super-busy pulling out an onion and peeling it. "Oooh," he says, swiping at his eyes, "chopping onions always makes me cry."

Great. Obviously my dad and Cindy have had some kind of clandestine dinner involving pot roast. And they didn't tell me about it. Which means that there had to be some kind of reason they didn't want me to know. Was it a date? Are Cindy and my dad having secret dates together? This is way too much for me to process.

"Cindy," I say hopefully, "don't you think we should have pizza? Or maybe tacos or something?"

She frowns. "Why would we do that when your dad is making pot roast?"

Oh, for the love of . . . "Well, because it's supposed to be a *party*. You know, and pot roast isn't exactly that much of a party food."

"Pot roast is perfect for a dinner party," she says. "And don't worry, your friends will love it."

Great. When it comes right down to it, Cindy is totally loyal to my dad. Either that or completely clueless. I should have known. "I'm going to take a shower," I announce. When I leave the kitchen, they're chopping potatoes and Cindy's still giggling.

I take a bath instead of a shower and stay in there so long, reading and soaking in my honey wheat vanilla bubble bath, that my fingers get all pruney. But my skin is super-soft and my hair smells delish. Hopefully this will be enough to distract Brandon from the fact that we're having pot roast.

I dry my hair, use my straightening iron, curl the ends, and then finally weave the strands of sparkly heart jewelry into my hair. It looks fab. Very festive and very hip. I have to be super-careful when I get dressed, though, because pulling my shirt over my head has the potential to really mess it all up. I should have gotten dressed before I did my hair, but then I would have had to wear my outfit for way too long. What if it got wrinkled, or I spilled eye shadow on it or something?

After I'm dressed, I carefully apply some sparkly lip gloss to make my lips totally kissable, then fasten a silver heart necklace around my neck. I slide my feet into my ballet flats and survey the result in the mirror. So. Cute.

As if on cue the doorbell rings, and I rush downstairs just in time to see Cindy opening the door. Ellie, Kyle, and Brandon are all standing on the steps.

"Hi, guys," I say.

"Hi!" Ellie says. I invite them in, and then introduce them to Cindy.

"Dinner's almost ready!" my dad calls from the kitchen.

"I'm starving!" Kyle yells back. "Is it pizza?"

Great.

Twenty minutes later we're all sitting around the kitchen table, and, um, it's not going that well. The pot roast is good, but it's, you know, *pot roast*. Also, my dad has this whole thing about mashed potatoes and how you mash them at the very last minute and then bring the pot over and put a big dollop on everyone's plate. It has something to do with the potatoes not getting hard, which is kind of an unnecessary worry. I mean, I don't think this crowd is really going to be worried about things like that.

Anyway, when my dad tried to bring the potatoes over to the table, he dropped them. And mashed potatoes splattered all over the floor. And Ellie started laughing, and then so did I (because once *she* starts laughing, I usually start laughing), which I don't think my dad appreciated. And then Kyle was like, "It's okay, Mr. Williams. I don't mind eating them!" And then he reached over and grabbed his spoon and scooped up some potatoes from the floor and popped them into his mouth. "Delicious," he said, and then took another scoop. I think he was doing it just be nice, but still.

Cindy looked like she was going to flip out and/or be sick.

So then my dad was like, "No, it's okay. We have some instant ones." And so then everyone had to wait while my dad made instant potatoes on the stove. It was super-awkward, you know, because no one really knew what to say. And at that point no one even really *wanted* the potatoes, but we had to wait anyway because it was so obvious that my dad was all upset. And by the time the instant potatoes were done, all the other food was cold. Honestly, it was kind of a debacle.

"So," my dad says now as he scoops big bunches of instant potatoes onto all of our plates. He somehow read the directions on the package wrong and ended up making, like, twenty-four servings. So now he's giving everyone way more potatoes than they're going to be able to eat. "Time to dig in!"

Kyle picks up his fork and takes a taste of potatoes. "Instant is definitely not as good," he says sadly.

"So, Brandon," Cindy says, serving herself some pot roast. "Do you play any sports?"

"Baseball," Brandon says.

"Oh, really?" my dad says. "I used to play baseball. What position do you play?"

"Catcher."

"Catcher? We used to say the catcher was nothing but a place for the pitcher to throw the ball." He laughs, but it's actually not that funny of a joke, and it's also pretty insulting at the same time.

"Do you have any ketchup?" Kyle asks. "I like to have ketchup on my pot roast."

My dad looks at him like he's lost his mind. But then Cindy says, "Of course. I'll get it." But I don't want her getting the ketchup in my house, because why should she? She doesn't live here, and besides, they're *my* guests.

So I get up to go and get the ketchup, but when I push my chair back, I somehow end up slamming my chair into Brandon's fingers. I don't even know how it happens, but he screams, "Ow!" and my dad looks up and gives Brandon a look like maybe he's overreacting.

"So!" Ellie says brightly. "Did you tell your dad about how well you did on your math test?"

"I did great on my math test," I say, opening the refrigerator and pulling out the ketchup.

"That's amazing, honey," my dad says.

"Yup," Brandon says. "I always knew she could do it." I feel myself blush. How sweet!

"No offense, Brandon," my dad says, giving him a smile, "but you do know that you helping Kendall isn't the only reason she got that good grade."

"Yes, sir," Brandon says. He looks a little scared now. I put the ketchup on the table in front of Kyle and slide back into my seat.

"Especially when you're studying at the mall," my dad goes on. He puts another big scoop of mashed potatoes on Brandon's plate. "I think we can all agree that's not really the best environment to focus in."

"Well, it must be working," I say, "since I'm doing so well."

"This pot roast is absolutely amazing," Kyle says. "Do you use a garlic rub?"

"Yes," my dad says proudly. "I buy a prepackaged one and then tweak it."

"Smart," Kyle says. He drags a big slab of roast through the pile of ketchup on his plate.

As if all of this isn't going horribly enough, Daniella picks that moment to pop up. "Wow," she says, surveying the scene. "This dinner party looks like a disaster." She wrinkles up her nose. "And who decided to have pot roast? Tacos would have been way better. Oooh, or make your own pizzas!"

I don't say anything. And then she bends down to whisper into my ear, which is ridiculous, since no one else can even hear her. "Kendall," she says, "I figured it out. Everything! I know what happened with me and Jen."

Chapter

12

I'm so startled that I drop the serving fork as I'm going to put it back on the pot roast plate. I didn't even want more pot roast. I was just doing it to make my dad feel better, but when I drop the fork, it goes into my chocolate milk. And chocolate milk goes running and dripping everywhere, including onto Brandon's jeans. Oops.

"Oh no!" I exclaim.

"Wow," Daniella says. "What a klutz."

"It's okay," Cindy says. She hops up from the table and grabs a dish towel. "No use crying over spilled milk." She forces a laugh.

"No," I want to say, "but you *can* cry over the biggest disaster of a date in your life." And if Brandon wasn't sure about being my boyfriend before, there's no way he's going to be super-psyched about it now.

I take the dishcloth from Cindy and crawl down under the table to wipe up the milk on the floor, but also so that no one will see that I'm about to start crying. Ellie will know, of course, since Ellie always knows when I'm about to start crying.

"Anyway," Daniella says, crawling under the table with me. God, she's flexible. I mean, there's hardly any room under here. "I remember now! About the digging!"

I stare at her blankly. "You remember about the digging?"

"Yes! We buried something!"

"You buried something?"

"Yes," she says. "I don't know what. Or where." She shakes her head and then smiles. "But that's really not important, since I'm sure we can figure it out. Maybe you can ask Jen."

"Ask *Jen*?" Suddenly all my frustration is coming out. About this disastrous dinner, about Daniella, about Mrs. Dunham, about everything. "Are you *crazy*? Did you miss the part where she said she was going to get a restraining order on me?"

"She did not," Daniella says, and rolls her eyes. "Don't be so dramatic."

"Who are you talking to?" Brandon asks. He has the tablecloth pulled up, and he's looking down at me, a worried look on his face.

"Um, no one," I say, and quickly stand up.

"I just heard you, though," Brandon says. "You were talking to someone."

"No, I wasn't," I say, smiling. "I'm fine. You must have been hearing things." Hopefully he doesn't remember the other day in math, when he also heard me talking to myself. Well, not myself. Daniella. But still.

"Probably," Brandon says. But he doesn't look convinced.

The rest of the night is pretty much a complete and total disaster. Kyle and my dad at least fill the silence by talking about recipes (turns out Kyle loves to cook, which Ellie thinks is adorable—I know because she's beaming at him the whole time), and then finally everyone goes home.

People shouldn't have gone home at eight o'clock on a Saturday! They should have hung around until at least nine or something. I even brought out that game Catch Phrase, but when I asked if anyone wanted to play, people took one look at Cindy settling in on the couch, and then Brandon was all, "Oh, I'm sorry, but I texted my mom already and she's on the way to pick us up."

I'm not sure if it was my imagination, but I felt like he was acting weird after he caught me talking to Daniella under the table. I mean, I thought I was being quiet, but I guess when I got emotional, I got a little loud.

Sigh. After everyone leaves, and my dad and Cindy

settle down in the living room with cups of coffee and chocolate chip cookies, I head upstairs and change into pajama pants and a long tank top. Then I take the heart jewels out of my hair, brush it until it's smooth, and pull it back into a plain ponytail. I wash my face with my special peach scrubbing facial wash and climb into my bed. I just want to fall asleep and forget all about this night.

But Daniella has other ideas.

"You're not lying in bed feeling sorry for yourself, are you?" she asks.

"Yes," I say, "I am. And I don't feel like talking, thank you very much." I don't say that if I *did* feel like talking, it certainly wouldn't be to her. It would be to Ellie, who texted me as soon as she left to see if I was okay. And I said I was, but that I didn't really want to talk too much right now, and that I would text her later. Which she totally understood. Because she's a good friend.

"Well, you don't have to," Daniella says.

"Thank you." I roll over in my bed so that my back is to her. "I appreciate your understanding." I expect her to go away, but after a couple of minutes I can still feel her there. So I turn around. She's doing a headstand against the far wall of my room. "Go. Away."

"That's not nice," Daniella says. She comes over and sits down at the foot of my bed. "Come on," she says. "I know just what you need."

She convinces me, somehow, that we have to go to the cemetery. She says it will cheer me up. It's late, and it's dark and kind of cold out, but I do need to clear my head, and walking in the cemetery does always calm me.

My dad's still in the living room with Cindy, and I don't tell him I'm going out, mostly because I don't want him to say it's too late. Instead I write a note and leave it on the kitchen table, telling him that I went for a walk and that I'll be home soon and he can text or call me if he needs me.

Then I grab my coat and slip out the door.

The cool air immediately starts to make me feel better, and I do my best to push out of my mind all thoughts of how tonight's craziness probably ruined my chances with Brandon.

Daniella, for once, is silent while we walk, but when we get to my usual bench, she looks at me and says, "Aren't you freaked out, being here at night by yourself?"

"No." I shrug and reach into my pockets, pulling out my fluffy white gloves and sliding my fingers into them. "What's to be scared of?"

"Well, *I'm* not scared," she says, "but I'm dead. Nothing really worse can happen to me, you know?"

"Nothing bad can happen to me either," I point out. "I can see ghosts. I can talk to them. I know they're not going to do anything horrible. If anything, they should be afraid of me, especially with the mood I'm in right now."

"Yikes," Daniella says.

We sit there for a while, not saying anything, just looking around. And then Daniella says, "So me and Jen buried something."

"So you said."

"Yup, me and Jen. We buried something here, at the cemetery."

"You buried something *at the cemetery*?" Is she crazy? That's, like, so illegal.

"Yes."

"And you have no idea where?"

"No."

"But you know that it's important that we find it so that you can move on?"

"Yes."

"Great." How the heck am I going to do *that*?

There's only one thing to do. I enlist Ellie to help me dig up the cemetery.

"You want me to help you do *what*?" she cries at school on Monday morning.

"I need to find something that I lost," I explain. I'm digging around (ha-ha!) in my locker, looking for a hair clip. I overslept this morning, and I had no time to do my hair. So I figured that I could put a hair clip in, sweep my hair to one side, and keep it kind of disheveled. Kind of like how I feel right now. Disheveled and out of sorts.

"You lost something in the cemetery?"

"No," I say. "Well, sort of. I buried something there."

"Like a treasure?" she asks, frowning.

"No, like a . . . I can't remember."

"Kendall, are you okay?" Ellie asks. She looks at me, concerned. "Is this whole Brandon thing throwing you for a loop? Because honestly, he's not worth it."

"Why?" I ask immediately. "What did he say?"

"Nothing," she says. And then she gets busy fiddling with the bottom of her shirt.

"Ellie," I say, taking a deep breath and putting my hands on my hips. "What. Did. He. Say?"

"Well, *I* didn't hear him say anything," she says, "but he told Kyle that you've been acting weird lately."

"I can't believe he said that," I say. I haven't been acting weird! I mean, just because I keep asking him about the color green, and just because he caught me talking to myself a couple of times, and just because I went to a gymnastics meet where I wasn't actually friends with anyone on the team, that doesn't mean that Brandon has to jump to all sorts of conclusions.

"Well, no offense, Kendall, but you have been acting kind of strange lately." Ellie looks at me. "Talking to yourself, being on edge all the time. What are you so nervous about? Does it have to do with your dad and Cindy?"

"My dad and Cindy?" Why would Ellie think it has anything to do with them?

"Yeah. Is it weird that they're getting so close?" She lowers her voice a little, because it's almost time for the bell to ring for homeroom, and the hall's getting pretty crowded. I guess she doesn't want anyone to hear.

God, Ellie's such a good friend. My stomach flips, and I think about how badly I wish I could just tell her about the ghosts. But instead I just say, "My dad and Cindy aren't getting close." Which is kind of true and kind of not. I mean, they're not, like, dating or anything. But I guess they are kind of getting close in the sense that they're . . . well, hanging out a lot. Cindy was over until really late on Saturday night. Not to mention their secret pot roast dinner.

"Okay," Ellie says. But she says it more like, *Oh, look. Kendall's in denial about her dad and Cindy,* instead of like she actually believes me. And then I realize that this is a chance for me to be resourceful.

So I hang my head and say, "Actually, Ellie, you're right. It could definitely be about my dad and Cindy. It's just really hard, you know, my dad hanging out with her, especially since I've never even really known my mom." Ellie reaches out and squeezes my arm, and I feel horrible for lying to her. But I can't have her thinking I'm some kind of lunatic.

"It's going to be fine," Ellie says. "I promise."

"Yeah," I say. But I'm not so sure.

Brandon is kind of . . . distant in school. He's not exactly unfriendly, but he's also not really friendly either. He's nice. And polite. But he was definitely a lot nicer to me before he came over to my house and caught me on the floor under my table, talking to myself and acting crazy.

A breakdown of our interactions in math:

ME: Hi, Brandon.

BRANDON: Hi, Kendall. (Smiles, but then sits in his seat and faces forward, effectively ending the conversation.)

ME (not giving up): Sorry about that dinner. My dad's not usually so overbearing. (Lie, lie, lie.)

BRANDON: It was fine. (He turns around and smiles again when he says this, but I can tell that it's not really that fine. His smile doesn't reach his eyes, and his tone sounds strained.) I had fun.

ME (knowing that he's lying): Yeah, well, I'd love a chance to make it up to you. (Random side note: I cannot believe I said that. I somehow morphed into crazy forward dating girl. But I couldn't help it! I like him! And why should the fact that I see ghosts and that my dad's a little overprotective wreck that for me? Isn't that like some kind of discrimination or something?)

BRANDON: Yeah, definitely. I'm kind of busy this week, but I'll text you.

ME (knowing when someone's blowing me off): Oh, okay. Cool.

In the halls between third and fourth, passing by each other:

BRANDON: Hi.
ME: Hi.

At lunch:

KYLE: Kendall, are you going to eat your bologna sandwich?

ME (slightly miserable): No, take it.

KYLE (starts to eat sandwich): This is delicious. Did your dad make it?

ME: No. I did.

(Ellie gives pointed look to Kyle.)

KYLE (slows down eating, then wipes his mouth): Thank you so much, Kendall. I really appreciate you sharing your sandwich with me.

BRANDON (packing up the rest of his lunch): So, I
    should get down to Mr. Jacobi's room. I need to
    ask him a question about math club.

ME: I didn't know you were going to be in math
    club.

BRANDON: I'm not. I mean, I can't, because of base-
    ball. The math club has most of their meets in
    the spring. But Mr. Jacobi wants me to, so I have
    to talk to him about it.

ME: Oh.

(Brandon leaves, and I have to spend the rest of
lunch with Ellie and Kyle holding hands and making goo-goo eyes at each other. Ugh.)

"You're not going to just give up that easily, are you?" Daniella yells. It's later that afternoon, and she's in my closet,
looking at all my clothes. "You need to get a cute outfit on
and go after him! Get him back! Right this instant! Come
on, let's go!"

"Daniella, I don't even know where he is," I say. "And
besides, even if I did, I can't stalk him like that."

"It's not *stalking*," she says. "It's like that time when
Lewis Marchone thought he didn't want to take me to the
junior prom because I was a freshman. He just needed a
little convincing." She nods emphatically, probably remem-

bering some crazy stunt she pulled to get him to ask her.

"You went to the junior prom with a boy named Lewis?"

"Shut up," she says. "You should wear your black skirt with your white—" And then suddenly her face goes pale. "Oh my God," she says, and her hands fly up to her face. "I just remembered something."

"What now?" I'm so not in the mood to deal with this. In fact, if I'm being completely honest, I'm starting to wonder if I should even really be talking to Daniella. Like, at all. Now that I'm in seventh grade and this whole talking-to-ghosts thing is starting to interfere with my social life, I'm beginning to think it might be time to retire. I want the ghosts to be able to move on, I really do, but I've been helping them for years, and I can't just give up my entire life for them. At some point I have to start looking out for myself.

"We . . ." She falls down to the floor. "We buried something. In the cemetery."

"I know," I say. "And we've been through this. I can't just go around digging up the cemetery." The more I thought about it, the more I started to think that digging up the cemetery was so not a good idea. I mean, it would have been one thing if Ellie had agreed to help. Then we could have pretended it was some kind of fun adventure. But after seeing her reaction, I realized what a completely dumb idea it is. I really don't need to get arrested.

"Not 'dig up,'" Daniella says. "We probably didn't dig all that deep. We just probably dug a little bit down and then dropped whatever it was into the ground." She bites her lip. "It was something shiny. Something important. If you found it, I know Jen would believe that you and I were friends."

"I don't have a shovel," I say. It's true. Even if I wanted to dig up the cemetery (which I don't), I don't have the proper tools.

"Your dad does."

"How do you know?"

"Kendall, I've been all over your house." She rolls her eyes, like she can't believe how naïve I am.

"That's creepy," I say, imagining her floating all around the house while we sleep at night, checking out all our things. At least she can't touch anything. Or turn the pages of my notebooks.

"And seeing ghosts isn't?"

"Good point."

"Commme oonn," she says. She throws herself down onto my bedroom floor dramatically. "Don't you want to get rid of me?"

"Another good point. However, digging up the cemetery is illegal."

"It is?" She bites her lip and bats her eyelashes at me.

"Yes," I say, turning back to my computer. "And while that look might have worked on Lewis, it isn't going to work on me. We are not digging up the cemetery."

"But they bury people there! How can digging be so wrong?"

"Yeah, they bury people there, but you can't just go around digging things up yourself." I swivel back around on my desk chair and look at her, my eyes wide. "Besides, what if we were digging and we dug up some bones?" How scary would that be? Ghosts are one thing. Their remains are another. I shiver, imagining all kinds of decaying bones and skulls caked with dirt.

"We won't dig up any bones," she says, rolling her eyes. "Jen and I didn't. I'd remember something as traumatic as that, for sure."

"But you and Jen were digging somewhere you knew," I say. "You want me to just go and start digging up the land in random places. Random places that could have *skeletons*."

"We'll stay away from the graves," she says, like it's that easy.

"Oh, right," I say. "Good idea. But what if the graves are wrong? Like, what if back in the 1800s or something they didn't mark them right? Or what if they've had so many bodies since then that now they just, like, I don't know, double-bury them, and when we bring our shovel out there, we're going to be digging and then all of a sudden we'll hit on something and we'll—"

"Kendall!"

"Okay, fine," I grumble. "I'll make you a deal. I'll try to dig something up at the cemetery tomorrow."

"Yay!"

"*But* you need to stay away from me and Brandon while I'm trying to see if we still have a chance."

"Deal," she says. Now I just need to come up with some kind of brilliant plan to see if Brandon and I *do* have a chance.

Chapter

13

"Okay," Ellie says the next morning. We're standing outside of school on the sidewalk in front of the buses. She puts her hands on my shoulders and looks me in the eye. "Do you remember what we talked about?"

"Yes," I say. "I'm going to go in there and be completely normal whenever I see Brandon."

"Completely normal," she says. "No thinking about your dad and Cindy."

"No thinking about my dad and Cindy," I agree. Which will be easy, because obviously I'm not even thinking about my dad and Cindy. And it will be easy to be normal, because Daniella is sticking to her promise, and she has stayed away. I don't know how long that will last, but for now it's good. I'm totally determined not to get all anxious and nervous. "How do I look?" I ask Ellie.

I do a little twirl. I'm wearing a pair of black skinny jeans, a black and white striped top, black shoes with a low heel, and for a touch of color I borrowed this really amazing shimmery red scarf from Ellie, which I've wrapped around my neck in a very cool way. My hair is in a side pony, and I have face shimmer brushed across my cheeks, and the perfect amount of lip gloss on my lips.

"You look amazing," she says. "Now let's go find the boys."

The boys are leaning against Ellie's locker, so we don't actually even have that far to go. It's so cute that Kyle is waiting for her, the way boyfriends do. And it's just a plus that Brandon's there, keeping Kyle company.

It's still so weird, thinking that Ellie has a boyfriend. I never thought she'd have a boyfriend. She loved going through crushes like they were nothing. And I never thought the person who would make her stop doing that would be Kyle. I guess love really is blind.

Although, if that's true . . . does that mean Brandon doesn't like me that much? Because if he did, wouldn't he accept the fact that I'm a little, uh, quirky and just be like, "Oh, that's just Kendall, ha-ha, I really like her so much"?

"Hi, boys," Ellie says. Wow. She sounded very flirty when she said that. I might need to start taking lessons from her. I copy the way she's standing, with one foot angled toward her locker.

"Hey," Brandon says.

"Hi," Kyle says. He leans in and brushes his lips against Ellie's, and then they both blush bright red. God, those two are so cute together!

"What are you doing?" Ellie asks.

"Waiting for you," Kyle says. Wow. I guess he's been working on his flirting skills too.

"Um, I have to get to homeroom," Brandon says.

I shoot Ellie a panicked look. How am I supposed to practice being normal and keeping control of my nerves if Brandon is avoiding me? Luckily, Ellie saves the day. "Wait!" she yells. Brandon looks startled. "Um, I mean," Ellie says, lowering her voice, "before you go, I was wondering if you guys wanted to go ice-skating this afternoon."

"Ice-skating?" Brandon asks.

"Ice-skating?" Kyle asks.

"Ice-skating?" I ask. I know of no such ice-skating plan. Why didn't Ellie bring this up when we were coming up with our strategy earlier? I can't go ice-skating today. I have to dig up the cemetery.

"Yeah, ice-skating," Ellie says, elbowing me. "It'll be fun. They have open skate at the Walden Rink at four o'clock."

"I'm in," Kyle says. "I haven't skated in forever."

I look at Brandon. Brandon looks at me. I don't want to say that I want to go, because then what if he says he's *not* going? Then not only will I know that he doesn't want to go because I'm going, but I'll be stuck going with Ellie and Kyle, and then I'll be the third-wheel loser who couldn't get a date.

"Bran?" Kyle asks. "My mom can probably drive you."

Brandon hesitates and I hold my breath. And then he finally says, "Yeah, okay. I'll go."

My breath comes rushing out of my in one big whoosh. "Me too."

Daniella will just have to deal.

But Daniella is not, um, really that good at dealing.

"You're doing *what*?" she screeches at the end of the day. I'm at my locker, loading up my bag with the books I need for my homework tonight.

"I'm going ice-skating with Ellie and Kyle and Brandon," I say. "Daniella, I had to! It's my only chance to make Brandon see that I'm not a total freak with a father who wants to kill him if he even looks at me."

"But this is my only chance to move on!" She puts her hands on her hips and stamps her foot. "Moving on trumps dating drama."

"No, it doesn't," I say, "and it's not your only chance. Don't be so dramatic. Anyway, it's probably going to take forever to dig up whatever magical item it is you think is going to help you."

"That's not true," she says, glaring at me. "And even if it is going to take forever, then the sooner we get started, the better."

I'm walking down the hall now, toward the front door of the school, where Kyle's mom is picking us all up and driving us to the ice-skating rink. My dad's going to drive us home, which could definitely be awkward, but I'll deal with that when it happens.

"Look," I say, "I'm sorry, but I have a life too. You can't just come in here and disrupt things, thinking I'm going to drop everything to—"

"I think," she says, cutting me off, "that me getting out of limbo or wherever it is that I'm stuck is a little more important than your dumb middle school romance. And besides, we had a deal."

"It's not a dumb romance," I say, "and just fyi, you're being pretty mean. You don't rule my life, Daniella. And if you keep acting like you do, you might have to find someone else to help you move on."

This must really make her mad, because she disappears. And then I do feel kind of bad, because we *did* have a deal. I'm about to call her name and see if she'll come back, but then Brandon is standing behind me.

"Hey," he says, looking around, "who were you talking to?"

• • •

Okay, so that was a little bit awkward. I mean, I'm supposed to be convincing Brandon that I'm normal, not that I'm even crazier than he first thought. So I told him that I'm going to be in the school play and that I was practicing my monologue. And then he said that he didn't even know there was going to be a school play, and so then I told him I didn't either but at some point there would be, and I wanted to be prepared.

"Ellie," I whisper as we walk down the sidewalk toward Kyle's mom's car. "When we get in the car, make sure you mention how I've always wanted to be an actress."

"*What?*" Ellie's eyes are about to bug out of her head, probably because the last time I tried to be an actress was in second grade when we did the Christmas play and I ran off the stage in the middle of the performance because I had such bad stage fright.

"Just do it," I say as we all pile into Kyle's mom's car. Kyle sits in front. And me, Ellie, and Brandon sit in the back, with Brandon in the middle.

"So how are you doing with working toward your dream of becoming an actress?" Ellie asks once we've said hello to Kyle's mom and we're pulling out onto the highway.

"Very good," I say, nodding. "I'm going to be trying out for the school play."

"What school play?" Ellie asks. I shoot her a look.

"Oh, right, the school play that's coming up soon."

"I want to be in the play!" Kyle says. I didn't even know he was listening.

"Kyle, you have enough extracurricular activities," his mom says. "You need to focus on your grades."

"That's true," I say. "Grades are more important. Besides, I'm not exactly sure when the auditions are. I just, uh, heard some teachers talking and saying that they're going to be coming up soon."

"Kendall's working on her monologue," Brandon explains.

Ellie's eyes pop open really wide. "Your *monologue*?"

"Yes," I say, "I have to do a monologue. You know, at the audition."

"I used to love preparing monologues," Kyle's mom says. "It's so exciting, being up there on the stage all by yourself with the spotlight on you!" She sighs, like she's thinking about fond memories. Probably because her monologues were real and not fake.

"You were an actress, Mom?" Kyle asks. He reaches over and turns on the radio, scanning the channels for a good song. I cross my fingers, hoping that he turns it up loud enough so that we can't talk.

"Well, I was in a few plays in college." She looks at me in the rearview mirror. "Where's your monologue from, Kendall?"

"Um, it's . . ." I think about saying it's from *Romeo and Juliet*, because honestly that's the only play I can think of right now. I mean, it's totally famous. I wouldn't even know any other place to do a monologue from. But if I say *Romeo and Juliet*, I'm afraid Kyle's mom might ask me to do it, and then what would I do? I've never even read *Romeo and Juliet*. So I say, "It's an original piece."

"An *original piece*?" Ellie asks.

"Wow," Kyle's mom says. "That's very ambitious, Kendall."

Luckily we're pulling into the skating rink now, and I open the door and hop out to the parking lot before anyone can ask me to do a bit of my original monologue. We all troop inside, and on the way Ellie says, "What the heck is going on?"

"I'll explain later," I say, pasting a smile on my face.

We all rent skates from the front counter and then head out onto the rink.

Ellie and Kyle immediately grab hands and start skating, leaving me and Brandon standing there on the ice, looking at each other kind of awkwardly.

"So," I say brightly, "are you a good ice-skater?"

"Sort of," he says. "I played hockey, so I can at least stay up. But I can't do any tricks or anything. You?"

"Just spins," I say. I spin around to show him, pulling my hands in close to my body and going around and around and around. But when I come out of it, I'm a little bit dizzy, and so I stumble a little, and the toe pick of my skate gets caught on the ice.

"Whoa," Brandon says, putting his arms around me to stop me from falling. My face is buried in his puffy green coat, and I inhale his scent, not able to stop myself from thinking about what it would be like to kiss him.

"Sorry," I say, laughing and pulling back. "I guess I'm a little rustier than I thought."

"That's okay," he says, giving me a smile. "I thought it was great."

We start to skate around the rink at a steady pace, dodging in between the little kids going super-slow and the older kids, who are racing around like they're in the Indy 500. The ice goes scraping under our skates as we build up a little speed, and after a while we're skating pretty comfortably, without too many wobbles.

"So did you ever find out how you did on the math test?" he asks.

"Eighty-eight," I tell him proudly.

"Are you serious?"

"Yeah," I say, feeling myself blush even though my cheeks and nose are a little cold from being on the ice.

"That's so awesome." He puts his hand out to give me a high five, and I reach my mittened hand up to slap against his. But something about reaching for his hand makes me go a little off balance, and I stumble again. It's not as bad as the first time, so Brandon doesn't have to put his arms around me. But his fingers tighten around mine, and I use his grip to stabilize myself.

"You okay?" he asks.

"Yeah," I say. "Sorry. I don't know what's going on. I'm usually able to stay a lot more upright." He's still holding my hand. No wonder I'm sliding all over on my skates. I can't keep my stomach from flipping all around, and it's obviously interfering with my knees and legs.

We skate around for a little longer, still holding hands, and then we decide to hit the snack bar for a hot chocolate. We buy two steaming cups and an apple cider doughnut to share, then climb up the bleachers so that we can watch everyone else skate while we eat.

"What do you think of those two?" I ask Brandon, pointing as Kyle tries to do a backflip on the ice. His form is all wrong. Daniella would definitely have something to say about that.

"Kyle and Ellie?" Brandon asks. He breaks off a piece of our doughnut and hands it to me.

"Yeah."

"I think they're good together." I raise my eyebrows at him. "No, seriously, I do," he says. "I've never seen Kyle act so nice to a girl before."

"Really?"

"Yeah," he says. "I think he really likes her."

"I think she really likes him, too," I say. The moment is so perfect—watching my best friend skate with a guy she really likes, while I sit up in the bleachers with a guy *I* really like, a nice hot drink in my hand. I close my eyes and inhale the smell of the ice, feeling happy and content.

"Are you cold?" Brandon asks. Probably because I just kind of shivered, mostly because I was so happy and he was so close to me.

"A little," I say.

"Here." He takes his hat off and puts it on my head.

"Thanks," I say. And when he takes my hand again, I lean my head on his shoulder.

Chapter

14

Daniella's on the warpath. Big-time.

"You," she says, "are not a very good ghost talker or communicator or whisperer or whatever you want to call it." She's wagging her finger at me and getting really loud.

"Stop," I say. But I'm not too upset about her yelling at me, because all I can think about is how fun it was to go ice-skating with Brandon. He even let me keep his hat. Well, not forever. At least, I don't think. I'm going to give it back to him at school tomorrow. Yay! We're back on track! Ellie was right. All it took was a little fun and normal time for Brandon to realize how fun and amazing and smart I am. And now, hopefully, I'll be able to relax a little around him.

"No, I will not stop," Daniella says. We're in my room, and I'm lying on my bed, writing down in my journal everything that just happened at the ice-skating rink while Daniella continues her rant. I'm wearing a pair of comfy black yoga pants, a long-sleeved pink crew T-shirt, and a pair of soft and warm slipper socks. Brandon's hat is still on my head. I'm warm and toasty and starting to get sleepy.

"You were really mean to me earlier, and now you're being even meaner! If there were some kind of department or something I could report you to, I would," Daniella says. "I would report you immediately. I would tell them to take away your ghost license!"

"I don't have a ghost license," I say, rolling my eyes. "And if I did, I would love for you to report me. I wish it were that easy to stop having to see ghosts." Could you imagine? If that's how it worked, I could just ignore the ghosts until I got tons of complaints, and then they would go away.

"That's the problem," Daniella says. "You don't *have* to do anything I say. You don't *have* to help me. There's nothing in it for you, and . . . and . . . it's really hard being dead!" Her voice is starting to shake, and I look up from my notebook in alarm. I didn't want to make her feel so bad.

"Hey," I say, jumping off the bed. I can't hug her, of course, but I should at least try to make her feel better. "It's going to be okay."

"No, it isn't," she says. "I don't want to be here anymore,

and you . . . you . . . you don't even care about helping me!" She's really crying now. Like, sobbing uncontrollably. Yikes.

I sigh. "Fine," I say. "First thing in the morning we'll go over to the cemetery and start digging. Just please stop crying."

"No," she says, and swipes at her eyes. "Tomorrow's Wednesday. You have school in the morning."

"Not until eight," I say. "We'll get up at six."

"Do you promise?"

"Yes," I say. I feel horrible for blowing her off today and making her so sad. Like it or not, I'm the only one who can help Daniella. And it's my responsibility to try to make things right.

Of course, when my alarm goes off at five forty-five the next morning, I'm not feeling so charitable. I was in the middle of this delicious dream where I was Cinderella and Brandon was the prince, and I'd left my hat at the skating rink and he was riding all around town on a horse trying to find me and confess his true love.

I reach out and slam the off button on my clock, then bury my head in my pillow, hoping maybe Daniella forgot about our plan.

"Rise and shine!" she yells from the bottom of the bed.

"I'm awake," I grumble, even though I'm not.

"Come on, come on, come on." She's walking over me

now, which I can't really feel, but just the fact that she's doing it is enough to creep me out. I throw the covers onto the floor, then walk grumpily over to my closet. I pull a sweatshirt on over my pajamas, shove my feet into my boots, and grab my coat.

"You're not even going to brush your hair or anything?" Daniella asks. She looks at me and wrinkles her nose, like she can't believe what a mess I am.

"Why would I brush my hair?" I ask. "We're going digging. I'd just mess it all up." Even though she's a ghost, some people actually have to worry about getting dirt all over them.

"Well . . . then why aren't you wearing work clothes?"

"These are work clothes!"

"Those are yoga pants."

"Well, I can work in these. I've done lots of homework in these pants. Plus they're washable. I don't care if they get dirty." The truth is, I'm just too lazy and tired to change. And honestly, she should talk. She's been wearing the same gymnastics uniform for weeks.

"I guess," Daniella says, not seeming so sure.

We have to sneak out of the house so that my dad doesn't wake up, but I do stop in the garage on the way out to grab a shovel. I take some work gloves while I'm at it, figuring I might as well keep my hands protected. Who knows what kind of disgusting stuff is lurking in the dirt?

Probably worms and bugs and thorns. And maybe bones. I shiver and then push the thought out of my mind before I have a chance to really think about it.

We traipse over to the cemetery, and Daniella knows enough to stay quiet as we walk. The sun isn't quite up yet, but it's starting to peek over the tops of the trees, and a few birds are starting to chirp. It's actually kind of relaxing, and I feel my mood start to lift a little.

I mean, honestly, what's to be upset about? Everything is going well—my math grade is back on track, Brandon and I had a great date, Ellie and Kyle are happy. And my good luck continues, because once we get to the cemetery, Daniella says, "There." She points over to some roses.

"'There' what?"

"There's probably where we buried whatever it is."

"In the rosebushes?"

"I love roses," she says, and shrugs.

"So much that you'd dig them up?" Wow. Talk about being inconsiderate. I mean, those rosebushes are beautiful. Although, I guess she didn't do too much lasting damage, since the bushes look the same as always. But still. Probably someone had to come and replant them.

"So much that I'd bury something with my best friend there because I probably thought it was lucky or something," she says, acting like the answer should be obvious.

"Whatever," I say, not really sure I believe her. Also, if

anyone comes along and sees me digging up roses, it's definitely not going to go along with my story that I'm planting a bush for my dead grandmother, Cecilia C. Worthington. (Cecilia C. Worthington is so not my grandmother. She just happens to be the closest grave to the flowers that Daniella wants me to dig up.)

I stick the tip of my shovel into the ground. Luckily, the roses are forming a ring around a tall elm tree, and so I don't actually have to dig them up. That would be way too sad. And destructive. I just have to dig in the circle of dirt around the tree.

"How far down do you think you would have gone?" I ask.

"Probably not too far," she says. "I don't really like to get dirty." Somehow this doesn't surprise me.

I get to shoveling. But after about half an hour, I'm starting to think I've dug myself too deep. (Ha-ha, get it?) I haven't found anything, there's dirt all over the place, and I'm turning into a sweaty mess.

"You have dirt on your cheek," Daniella points out helpfully.

"Thanks," I say, and glare at her. I plop down on one of the big rocks that line the garden and swipe at my cheek with my hand. "Look," I say, "I'm sorry, but I have to go to school now. And I haven't found anything. So I think we should—"

And that's when I feel it. My foot brushing against something in the dirt. Something hard. I automatically jerk my foot back, all sorts of thoughts floating through my head about what it could be. *Please don't be a skeleton, please don't be a skeleton.* . . . I turn to look. But it's not bones. It's something shiny and metallic. The sun glints off the metal, and I reach down and pull it out of the dirt. It's a bracelet, and there's another one next to it. Two beaded silver friendship bracelets.

"Oh my God," Daniella says as soon as she sees it. "I remember! I remember the whole thing now. I know what happened." Her face has gone completely white, even whiter than usual. She's looks really upset, like she might start crying.

"What is it?" I ask. "Daniella, what happened?"

But before she can say anything, I hear a voice behind me.

"Kendall?" Brandon asks. "What are you doing?"

"What are you doing here?" I ask while quickly hopping out of the rosebushes. Or, uh, what used to be the rosebushes.

"I came to visit my mom's grave," he says. He's looking at the shovel with a weird look on his face.

"This early?"

"Sometimes I ride my bike over here before school."

"Cool. Me too. I mean, I walk here. To, uh, visit my

grandma's grave." I push my sweaty hair out of my face, then reach for the hair tie I always keep on my wrist. But it's not there. Crap. I must have lost it in the dirt somewhere. I scan the ground, but I don't see it. Not that it matters. There's no way I'd pick up some muddy hair tie and put it in my hair in front of Brandon.

"Okay." Brandon hesitates, and I think he's going to ask me why he's never seen me here in the morning before. But instead he says, "What are you doing, digging all around?"

"I'm planting a bush," I say. "A bush for my grandma."

"But there are already rosebushes here," he says. "And isn't your grandma's grave over there?" He looks concerned, like he knows what I'm doing is wrong and now he's going to have to make the hard choice about whether or not he wants to call law enforcement on me. But that's crazy. Brandon would never call the police on me. Brandon is in serious like with me. Isn't he?

"I know," I say. "But, ah, I . . . I was thinking I would plant something else."

"What were you going to plant?"

Good question. "Friendship bracelets!" I say brightly, holding them up.

"You were going to plant friendship bracelets in the cemetery?" He's looking at me like I'm crazy.

"Well," I say, "they're actually, you know, good luck. If you plant them. It's an ancient Chinese ritual."

Brandon moves forward and takes one of the friendship bracelets out of my hand and looks at it. "'Besties Forever,'" he reads. "These are good luck?"

Daniella guffaws.

"Yes," I say, "but, ah, I forgot the paper at home, the one that has the special, uh, Chinese prayer you're supposed to chant before you plant them. So I can't plant these right now."

"Okay." He opens his mouth like he wants to say something else, but then shuts it. He's silent for a second, and then he says, "So, ah, I guess I'll see you at school."

"Yup," I say, swiping at my face again for any stray dirt. "See you at school!"

I stand there for a while, waving at him with a big smile on my face so he doesn't realize anything's wrong. What the heck is Brandon doing, showing up everywhere I go? It's really too bad, because if he didn't keep catching me doing ridiculous things, I would think us running into each other meant something—that, like, we were destined to be or something. But obviously we're not, since all the normalness of yesterday's fab date just got erased. Sigh. If I hadn't ruined my chances with Brandon Dunham before, then that definitely just did it.

By the time school is over for the day, I'm exhausted. Who knew that all that digging would take so much out of me?

It's like that time when Ellie and I thought we'd try out for the track team, but then we went running for a couple of days to get ready and decided it just wasn't worth it.

Plus Brandon had a dentist appointment during math, and a baseball meeting during lunch, so not only did I not get to see him, I got stuck sitting with Kyle and Ellie all by myself. Ugh. Kyle kept feeding Ellie licorice, which was very annoying. I mean, I'm happy for them and everything, but shouldn't they know better than to do that kind of thing when other people are around?

Anyway, it's after school, and now I'm at the high school again, waiting outside for Jen to come out of her gymnastics practice. I have the bracelets I dug up this morning in my pocket. It's a little cold out here, so cold that I have to keep hopping from foot to foot to stay warm. But I'm afraid to go inside, because if Jen sees me at her practice before I have a chance to talk to her, who knows what she'll do? Get me kicked out at the least, call the police on me at the worst.

So I'm kind of, ah, hiding behind a bush when she finally comes walking out. Thank God she's alone. She's putting on a pair of really cute puffy purple gloves, and I fall into step behind her, la, la, la.

"Jen?" I try.

She turns around, a smile on her face, but when she sees me, her face darkens and she quickens her step. "You!"

she says. "Go away!" Wow. She sounds kind of like Mrs. Dunham. Why does everyone think it's okay to call me "you"? That's so rude.

Daniella pops up. "Where the heck have you been?" I say to her.

Jen thinks I'm talking to her, though, and so she turns around and says, "That's none of your business. You need to take a hint and leave me alone." She starts rummaging around in her bag, and for a second I think maybe she's going to pull out some kind of pepper spray or something. But she's just looking for her car keys.

"Wait!" I say. "Daniella told me about your friendship bracelets!" She keeps walking, and I'm not sure if it's my imagination, but I think I see her slow down just a little bit. "The ones you buried at the cemetery."

She whirls around then, her hair whipping against her face. "How did you know about that?"

I think about telling her again that Daniella's family was friends with mine, but at this point it doesn't matter. She isn't going to believe it, and besides, she doesn't have to.

I pull the bracelets out of my pocket and hold them up. I spent some time cleaning them off with my jewelry cleaner, and so they sparkle in the afternoon sun. "She told me about them," I say, "and I thought you might want them."

She reaches out to take them, and her eyes fill with tears. "You . . . How did you . . ."

"Tell her that I don't blame her," Daniella says. "Tell her I don't blame her for the fight we got into."

"Daniella wants you to know that she doesn't blame you," I say. "She says that she's not mad." I have no idea what it means, since isn't *Daniella* the one who took *Jen's* boyfriend? But whatever, I'm just the messenger.

Jen starts crying then. Her whole face crumples up, and tears run down her face. We're in the middle of the parking lot, and a couple of people turn to look as they walk by, but Jen doesn't seem to notice.

"I didn't mean it," she says. "I wanted to give her a ride, I did. I was just so mad at her for what she did with Travis. And so when she called to see what time I was picking her up, I told her she'd have to find her own way to the meet. And so she took the bus." She swipes at her tears with the back of her hand, and that's when I get it. Jen and Daniella got into a fight because Daniella was hanging out with the boy that Jen liked. And so Jen told Daniella to find herself another ride to the meet. And that's why Daniella was on the bus that ended up crashing.

"Tell her it's not her fault," Daniella says. "Please, please, please tell her it's not her fault." And now she's crying too.

"It's not your fault," I tell Jen. "Daniella doesn't blame you. She doesn't."

"How do you know?" she asks. Her eyes are shiny with tears, and her tone is pleading. I hesitate.

"The same way I knew about the friendship bracelets," I say finally. "And let's just leave it at that."

She looks at me, then nods, and before I know what she's doing, she's grabbed me into a hug. She holds on to me for a long moment, still crying. And I feel like I want to cry too. I'm thinking about Ellie and best friends and how they can get you through your dark times, how they're always there for you. How true friends will love you no matter what. I think again about telling Ellie about the ghosts, and realize that maybe I should. Ellie will understand. Ellie's amazing. I always want to make sure that in my friendships I have no regrets. This whole thing with Daniella and Jen has made me realize that.

"Thanks," Jen says, pulling back. Her eyes are still wet, but she has a smile on her face now.

"You're welcome," I say.

And when I turn around, Daniella is gone.

Chapter

15

Well. I kind of miss her. Daniella, I mean. She's only
been gone for half an hour or so, but just knowing that she's
not coming back is kind of sad. Especially since I didn't get to
say good-bye. That's just how it works out sometimes. Sigh.

After I finish up with Jen (who feels a lot better after
we talk for a little longer—she even put one of the friendship bracelets on her wrist, which really seemed to comfort her—yay me for doing something good!), I have to run
back to my school so that I can take the late bus home.
When I get to my house, my dad's not back from work yet,
so I make myself a snack of apples and peanut butter and
settle in the living room to do my homework and try to
keep my mind off Brandon.

The house is quiet without my dad here, and I'm a little afraid Mrs. Dunham is going to show up. So I put some music on my iPod and set it on its dock to break up the silence.

I'm halfway through my history reading when my phone rings. Ellie.

"Kendall!" she yells. "Where have you been? I've been trying to call you for an hour!"

"I'm right here," I say innocently. "What's up?"

"Why didn't you tell me that Brandon found you at the cemetery this morning, digging up flower beds?"

"I wasn't digging up flower beds!" I say. Jeez. Talk about being dramatic and starting rumors. I mean, I told him I was burying friendship bracelets.

"Well, that's what he told Kyle. Kendall, what the heck were you doing?"

I swallow. "Ellie," I say, and take a deep breath. "I . . ." I want to tell her. I do. About Daniella, about the ghosts, about digging up the graveyard, about everything. But the words seem like they're stuck on my tongue.

"What?" Ellie asks. "Kendall, what is it?" She sounds so worried that the guilt squeezes my stomach like a rubber band.

I let out my breath in one giant whoosh. I just can't do it. If I lost her, I don't know what I'd do.

So I explain to her about the friendship bracelets, about sending them to my grandma with a Chinese proverb. And Ellie doesn't even question it, because we've been friends for so long that she's used to me doing weird things. In fact, she kind of likes it. She even starts asking questions about different Chinese spells and if there's any that we can do together. It actually sounds kind of interesting, and I tell her that I don't know too much about it but we should check it out. That's before I remember that I made the whole thing up, which makes me feel even more guilty. But I'm sure there's something out there that's sort of like it. I make a mental note to google ancient Chinese burial spells.

"Anyway," I say, tapping my pen against the pages of my history book. "Tell me more about what Brandon said."

"Just that you were acting weird," she says. "Kendall, I think you should go and talk to him."

"Hmmm," I say. "Good idea."

"And try not to be so nervous! Remember how well things were going at the skating rink?"

"Yes."

"Okay, so I'll let you go."

"Why?"

"So you can go and call him!"

"Right *now*?"

"Yes, right now! You need to get back on track."

"I guess . . ."

"Kendall," she says, "go." And then she hangs up.

I decide to send Brandon a text instead of calling him, because I figure it's less intrusive.

Hey, I say. *What r u doing?*

Homework, comes the reply. *U?*

Same. Want company? I hold my breath and cross my fingers.

After a minute comes his reply. *Sure. Wanna come over?*

Sure.

He can't be too weirded out if he's inviting me over, right? I rebraid my hair and put on some lip gloss. I almost miss Daniella's little comments about how much I'm screwing things up with Brandon and how much of a ridiculous middle school drama my romance is. "Good luck, Daniella," I whisper, hoping that wherever she is, she can hear me.

I call my dad at work and ask him if I can go to Brandon's, and after he confirms that Brandon's dad will be there, he says yes. And he didn't even have to call Cindy this time! I consider it progress.

I decide to ride my bike to Brandon's, since it's a little too far to walk.

"Hey," I say when he opens the door.

"Hi." He looks cute and casual in a pair of jeans and a button-up white and gray shirt.

"I brought my math notes," I tell him as I step into his front hall and take my coat off. "So you can copy them."

"Thanks," he says. "I had a dentist appointment during math." He takes my coat and puts it on the coatrack. "Do you want a juice or something?"

"Sounds great."

"All my stuff's set up in the dining room," he says. "So you can go ahead and go in there. Dad and Grace are outside throwing the ball around, but they'll probably be in soon."

"Okay," I say. I head to the dining room and spread my stuff out on the table while Brandon goes to get the drinks. *Just relax,* I tell myself. Brandon doesn't *seem* freaked out about the whole digging-up-the-cemetery thing, but I'm sure he is. So I need to get things back on track. Again. It should be a lot easier this time, I tell myself, without Daniella around.

And that's when I see it. The piece of green paper. Sticking out of Brandon's book bag, which is sitting on the chair next to me. I can hear Brandon moving around in the kitchen, opening the refrigerator and getting glasses down from the cupboard.

I think about what Mrs. Dunham kept saying. About adding myself to the green paper. That *has* to be the paper. I mean, Brandon takes it with him everywhere. I wonder if I could just . . . take a look. It wouldn't really be snooping, because now that Daniella's gone, I might really have to help Brandon's mom move on soon. Looking at that paper would be more like doing something in the line of duty.

So before I can talk myself out of it, I reach in and pull the paper out of Brandon's bag. It looks like a letter. It *is* a letter. From Brandon's mom to him. It seems like something she wrote to him before she died. "*Dear Brandon,*" it starts, "*I wanted to take this opportunity to write down everything I want to tell you, in case someday I'm not there to tell you in person.*"

Wow. That is so sweet. I start to tear up a little bit, actually. Because it's just so sad. I hear Brandon's footsteps moving closer, and my heart starts to beat fast. I run my eyes quickly down the paper, scanning it for anything that might make me understand what Mrs. Dunham is talking about.

And that's when I come to the end of the paper. And I see that there's a list of things that Mrs. Dunham wants Brandon to stay away from. I don't have a chance to read all of it before I have to shove it back into his bag.

"Hey," Brandon says, walking back into the dining room and setting two glasses of juice down on the table. "Is apple okay? Grace drank the rest of the orange."

"Apple's great," I say, but my mind is racing. What the

heck could Mrs. Dunham be talking about? Why would she want me to be on her letter to Brandon?

And then I have a horrible thought. Is Mrs. Dunham . . . She can't mean that *I'm* something Brandon should stay away from, can she? *Add yourself to the green paper.* But that . . . that doesn't make any sense. Why would I have to stay away from Brandon so that Mrs. Dunham can move on?

"Everything okay?" Brandon asks.

"Yup," I say brightly, even though my stomach's in my shoes. "Everything's fine." I take a sip of my juice and give him a smile. My heart's beating so fast in my chest, I'm afraid he's going to be able to hear it. I look at the green paper, hoping he won't be able to tell that I just put it back into his bag. I'm not sure that it's sticking out exactly the way it was before. Crap. I want to reach out and push it back in, but I don't—

"So it was fun ice-skating yesterday," Brandon says, and sits down at the table next to me.

"Yeah," I say, "I had fun too." My head is spinning, and I open my math book. *Okay, Kendall,* I tell myself. *Calm down. There's no way Mrs. Dunham meant for you to stay away from Brandon. She doesn't even know you.*

"I've never had that much fun with a girl before," Brandon says shyly. He inches his chair closer to mine, and now our legs are touching under the dining room table. Ohmigod,

ohmigod, ohmigod. His closeness is enough to make me forget about Mrs. Dunham and that stupid green paper. I'm probably overreacting about it, anyway. I'm very dramatic when I want to be.

"Me neither. I mean, I've never had that much fun with a boy before." I twist my hands nervously in my lap. "And about this morning," I say, "at the graveyard—"

"Shhh," Brandon says, putting his finger to my lips. "You don't have to explain."

"I don't?"

"No," he says, and grins. "You definitely keep things interesting, Kendall Williams."

And then, before I even know what's happening, he's moving his lips toward mine. And the moment is perfect and right, and I move my lips up to meet his, and then he's kissing me. When we pull apart, he rests his forehead against mine, and I just stay there for a second, my eyes closed, enjoying how amazing this feels.

My first kiss! I can't wait to tell Ellie!

"So," Brandon says, pulling back. "Should we work on our math?"

"Sure," I say, trying to keep my voice calm. But inside, a million fireworks are going off inside me, like tiny little explosions. How am I supposed to work on math at a time like this? I kissed Brandon Dunham! And he likes that I'm so quirky! He said I keep things interesting!

I turn the page in my math book, wondering if I can get away with sending Ellie a text about what just happened without Brandon noticing.

And that's when I see her. Mrs. Dunham. Sitting across from us at the table. I give her a friendly smile, hoping now that she sees how much her son likes me, she'll be a little more friendly. But Mrs. Dunham doesn't smile back. In fact, all she does is glare. . . .

Check out Kendall's next adventure!

THE HARDER THE FALL
By Lauren Barnholdt

Okay. Everything is going to be fine. I just need to stop obsessing over all the crazy things that are happening to me, and just relax. Of course, this is easier said than done.

I mean, let's look at a quick recap of my life, shall we?

1. I can see ghosts. That, in and of itself, is completely scandalous. I'm only twelve! How am I supposed to be expected to deal with the pressures of helping ghosts move on to the other side? It would be a lot of work for a grown-up, even. I have my hands full just trying to get through seventh grade.

2. I have my first maybe-almost boyfriend, Brandon Dunham. Brandon is sweet and smart and very cute, and he helps me with my math whenever I need it. He even gave me my very first kiss ever. He is pretty much the exact kind of person you would want to be your first crush. But still. Having a maybe-almost boyfriend can be stressful.

3. Brandon Dunham's mom died when he was younger, and now she is one of the ghosts I can see. (See number one, above.) When she first appeared a couple of weeks ago, she kept going on and on about how I should add myself to the green paper. I had no idea what that meant until a few days ago, when I was at Brandon's house studying with him and I looked at the green paper he's always carrying around in his backpack. And it turns out that the green paper is a list of things his mother wrote to him before she died—a list of things she thinks he should stay away from.

I quickly figured out that the fact that Mrs. Dunham wants me to put myself on the green paper means that she doesn't want me dating Brandon. But why? And how am I going to help Mrs. Dunham move on if her unfinished business involves me staying away from her son?

Not that I think Brandon and I are, like, destined to be together or anything. I mean, we're only twelve. But still. You can see why I might be just a tad bit distracted, even though it's Sunday afternoon and I'm supposed to be relaxing and having a fun time, enjoying what's left of my weekend.

"What's going on?" my best friend Ellie asks me as we walk down Main Street. When the weather's nice, Ellie and I sometimes spend our Sundays down on Main Street. We buy fresh fruit salads and hot chocolates from Donelan's Market, look at all the different stationery at Poppy's Papeterie, and browse for cute hair accessories at Jasmine's Boutique.

(I'm a huge fan of hair accessories. I like to try to make sure my hairstyle matches my mood. Like today, for example. My hair is in lots of beachy waves around my shoulders, because I'm kind of feeling loose and up in the air.)

"Nothing's going on," I tell Ellie. Which is a lie. But I can't really tell her the truth. In fact, I can't tell anyone the truth. No one knows I can see ghosts. I wish I could tell Ellie, I really do. But I can't risk the fact that she might not believe me, or she might think that I'm crazy. I don't know what I would do if I ever lost her friendship.

"Are you sure?" Ellie asks. "Because you've been really—"

"Oh, look!" I exclaim, pointing to a storefront on

the corner. "There's a new salon opening up." They have a huge sign in the window that says ALL NAIL POLISH 50% OFF.

"Don't change the subject," Ellie says as I stop in front of the store and peer in the window.

"I'm not."

"Yes, you—"

But Ellie's cut off by a woman poking her head out of the door of the salon. "Hello, girls!" she chirps. She has short blond curly hair and she's wearing silver-and-turquoise rings on almost every finger.

Hmm. I'm not sure I'll be getting my hair done here. You can tell a lot about how good a place is at cutting hair from how their employees look. And this woman is in desperate need of . . . I don't know, exactly. Highlights. Or a brush.

"Welcome, girls, welcome!" she says, ushering us inside. "Welcome to the Serene Spa and Wellness Center."

I frown. The sign on the door says HAIRCUTS.

She must notice that we look confused, because she quickly rushes on. "We haven't had time to change our sign yet. We just recently decided to make this into a full-service spa." She throws her hand out in a flourish, like she's indicating how awesome the place is.

Ellie looks at me and raises her eyebrows. I know she's thinking the same thing I'm thinking. That this place definitely doesn't look like a full-service spa. Not that I really know what a full-service spa looks like. I mean, I've only seen them in movies.

But I'm pretty sure they include lots of white towels and well-dressed attendants ready to wait on you hand and foot and bring you whatever you desire, as long as it's good for you. Things like raspberry-flavored sparkling water and cherries dipped in dark chocolate. (Dark chocolate is totally good for you. It has, like, a million antioxidants.)

This place has none of those things. All it has is a reception desk, a few folding chairs scattered around the waiting room, and one nail station right at the back.

"Well," I say slowly. "We don't really need a full-service spa. Um, but maybe we could have a manicure."

"Of course!" the woman says, and leads us over to the nail station. She frowns. "We only have one manicure table," she says. "So one of you will have to wait." She pushes a stray curl off her forehead and smiles. "And the shipment of nail polishes that was supposed to come in yesterday never came, so we're a little limited in our selection."

"That's okay," I say, smiling nervously at Ellie, who doesn't look too happy. In fact, she looks like she wants to hightail it out of here. Ellie's a stickler when it comes to things like customer service. She'll totally leave a place if she feels like she's not getting good treatment.

Usually I agree with her, but how can I leave now? This

poor woman seems so excited to have us here. We're probably her first customers ever.

"I want orange nail polish," Ellie says firmly, which is kind of ridiculous, because she doesn't even like the color orange.

"That's wonderful!" Sharon says. "Because that's one of the colors we have."

"Oh, great news," I agree, pushing Ellie toward the uncomfortable-looking chair that's sitting in front of the nail station. "I'll just wait up front and read a magazine or something."

Usually when Ellie and I get our nails done, we sit next to each other and gossip about people at school. But like Sharon said, there's only one nail stand.

"*You're* going to be doing my nails?" Ellie asks Sharon skeptically.

"Yes." Sharon nods and sits down at the nail station. She goes to open a bottle of orange nail polish and almost spills it all over. Yikes. "I just got my nail tech certification a few days ago." She points up to the wall, where a certificate is hanging in a gold frame.

"You've only known how to do nails for *two days*?" Ellie asks.

"Oh, no. I've only been *certified* for two days. But I've practiced on loads of people." Sharon beams.

"Okay, well, see you in a few minutes!" I yell, and

then I head back to the waiting area before Ellie can change her mind. I'm sure she'll be fine. I mean, it's just nails. What's the worst that can happen? She gets a little nail polish on her?

We can't just leave and crush poor Sharon's dreams. What if we left and she started thinking she was the worst salon owner ever and that she should just give it up and go back to whatever her job was before? I really don't want that on my shoulders. And I doubt Ellie does either.

I grab a magazine and sit down in one of the folding chairs. I wonder how long it will take Ellie to get her nails done. I hope not that long. The smell of chemicals in this place is starting to give me a headache.

I pull my phone out and check to see if I have a text from Brandon. But there's nothing. I wonder if I should text him. Not that I have a reason to text him, but do I really need a reason? I could just be all casual and ask him about the math homework or something. Of course, he would probably see right through that. I don't want to play hard to get, but at the same time—

"Excuse me," a voice says. "But is this Sharon's Haircuts?"

I look up from my phone to see a girl standing in front of me. She has long wavy dark hair and bright blue eyes. Her skin is pale, and she has a lot of makeup on. Like, a *lot* of makeup—smoky purple eye shadow, bronzer, mascara, and a slick of bubble-gum-pink lip gloss. She's wearing a short black skirt, a hot pink top, patterned tights, and leg warmers.

"Well," I say, "I think that's what it used to be called. But now they've changed the name. They're a full-service spa now." I throw my hand out in a flourish, the same way Sharon did.

"A full-service *spa*?" the girl exclaims. "How the heck is she going to handle that?"

"Who?"

"Sharon."

"Oh!" I brighten. "Do you know her?" Maybe this girl will fill me in on this Sharon person's backstory. Like how she came to own this salon. Maybe there's something really juicy behind it.

"Yes." The girl sighs and flips her hair over her shoulder. "She's my mom."

"Wow," I say, "that's so cool, your mom starting her own salon. Does she give you free manicures and stuff?"

She looks at me like I've asked the most ridiculous question she's ever heard. "Of course not."

Right. Well, maybe her mom's one of those people who want their children to learn the ways of the world and work hard for things. Maybe Sharon was a doctor or something and she's totally rich and sunk her life savings into this place to follow her one true dream. And she doesn't want to spoil her daughter, so she makes her work for everything, even manicures at the salon that she owns.

"Good idea," I say. "It's always better to work for things in life. That's my motto." It's not really my motto, but whatever. It could be.

"Anyway," the girl says, shaking her head and looking at me like I'm crazy. She starts looking around, peering into the back. "What's she doing back there, anyway?"

"She's giving my friend a manicure," I say. And then I realize something. "Hey, are you going to be starting school with us?"

"Starting school with you?" Now she's looking at me like I'm even crazier than before. She's definitely a rich kid. They're always looking at you like you're crazy, even when you're saying something that's totally reasonable.

"Yeah," I say. "You just moved here, right? So you're probably going to be going to my school. What grade are you in?"

"Seventh."

"Me too! Maybe I can show you around."

She shakes her head. "You don't get it, do you?"

Okay, now she's gone a little too far. All I'm trying to do is be nice. Not to mention the fact that poor Ellie is back there with this girl's mom, probably getting orange nail polish splashed all over her.

"Never mind," I say, picking my magazine back up.

"Sorry for, like, trying to be nice." Not my wittiest retort, but it should get the job done.

"No." She shakes her head and then bites her lip, looking frustrated. "I'm not . . . I mean, I don't know how this works, exactly."

"How what works? Responding when someone's being nice to you? I'll tell you what you *don't* do—act all snotty."

"No." She shakes her head again. "I'm Lyra."

"Great," I say. "I'm Kendall."

She's looking at me expectantly. Okay, this is getting weird. Like, what is this girl's deal? Why is she out here, in her mom's hair salon, acting like she's never been here and staring at me like she's waiting for me to say something?

"Kendall?" Ellie calls, coming out from the back of the salon. She's holding her hands up. One of her hands has the nails painted orange, and the other hand has the nails painted blue. Which makes no sense.

"What happened to your nails?" I ask her.

"Oh." She looks down. "Um, they ran out of orange nail polish."

Wow. This place is a big disaster.

"Who were you talking to?" Ellie asks. She looks around the waiting area, her eyes sweeping right over the girl standing in front of me.

I'm about to tell Ellie not to be rude (although, let's face it, if Ellie's going to be rude to anyone, it should be Lyra—

I mean, she kind of deserves it) when a sick feeling rolls through my stomach.

"Now do you get it?" Lyra asks, crossing her arms over her chest and giving me a satisfied smile.

And then I do get it.

Ellie can't see Lyra.

Because Lyra is dead.

IF YOU ♥ THIS BOOK,
you'll love all the rest from

YOUR HOME AWAY FROM HOME:

AladdinMix.com

HERE YOU'LL GET:

- ♥ The first look at new releases
- ♥ Chapter excerpts from all the Aladdin M!X books
- ♥ Videos of your fave authors being interviewed

Aladdin ♥ Simon & Schuster Children's Publishing ♥ KIDS.SimonandSchuster.com

Sometimes a girl just needs a good book.
Lauren Barnholdt understands.

www.laurenbarnholdt.com

EBOOK EDITIONS ALSO AVAILABLE

From Aladdin M!X   KIDS.SimonandSchuster.com

DOUBLE TROUBLE
JUST TOOK ON A WHOLE
new meaning....

EBOOK EDITIONS ALSO AVAILABLE
FROM ALADDIN
KIDS.SimonandSchuster.com

Real life. Real you.

seeing cinderella

Don't miss
any of these
terrific
Aladdin M!X
books.

CANTERWOOD
CREST
SUPER SPECIAL

CHOSEN
JESSICA BURKHART

TRAUMA
QUEEN
Barbara Dee

LAUREN BARNHOLDT

DEVON
DELANEY
SHOULD
TOTALLY
KNOW
BETTER

Odd Girl In
Jo Whittemore

Stealing
TRUDI
TRUEIT Popular

EBOOK EDITIONS ALSO AVAILABLE | KIDS.SimonandSchuster.com

Did you **LOVE** this book?

Want to get access to
great books for **FREE?**

Join

Simon & Schuster IN THE **bookloop**

where you can

✴ **Read great books for FREE!** ✴

💧 **Get exclusive excerpts** 💧

⧛ **Chat with your friends** ⧚

Log on to join now!

⧉ everloop.com/loops/in-the-book